SIXTY-FIVE
STIRRUP IRON ROAD

Brian Keene   J. F. Gonzalez   Nate Southard

Jack Ketchum   Bryan Smith   Ryan Harding

Edward Lee   Wrath James White   Shane McKenzie

deadite
press

deadite press

DEADITE PRESS
205 NE BRYANT
PORTLAND, OR 97211
www.DEADITEPRESS.com

AN ERASERHEAD PRESS COMPANY
www.ERASERHEADPRESS.com

ISBN: 978-1-62105-131-2

Acknowledgments

The authors would like to collectively thank Tom Piccirilli, Michelle Scalise, Jeff Burk, Rose O'Keefe, Carlton Mellick, Alan M. Clark, and the staffs of Deadite Press and Sinister Grin Press.

Extra-special thanks to Monica J. O'Rourke, Mark "Dezm" Sylva, Tod Clark, and Stephen "Macker" McDornell for their invaluable help with this project.

For Tom Piccirilli ...

PROLOGUE
EDWARD LEE

The taste was unmistakable; there could be no doubt—not to a palate with Nicci's incontestable track record.

It was the taste of sperm.

That FUCKER! she thought in a blare like a mental truck horn. The acknowledgment sprang her bolt-upright in bed. She smacked her lips, gagged, grimaced, and then—

Kurrrrrrr-HOCK!

—spat with a vengeance right onto the carpet. Appalled, she clicked on the light.

Did he really ... could he possibly have...? The actuality of what she suspected seemed—now that she'd been awake for several moments—*incredulous.* Couldn't it be, instead, that the awful, awful taste in her mouth was something else? Nasal drip? Cottonmouth from the eight beers she'd chugged while Sam was at work? Or a tiny burp of bile that had come up in her sleep? After all, she'd had the rest of the leftover kung pao that had been in the fridge for a few days. Nicci hoped for all she was worth that something like this was the case, but ...

But ...

For fuck's sake. Who am I kidding? If anybody knows what cum tastes like, it's me.

Yes, it was she, all right. If anyone knew, it was Nicci. Her indoctrination into fellatio as a means of boosting her income had been gradual. A blowjob or two per week at fifteen or twenty a pop really helped out. She'd do mainly dorky mall guys after work: the security guard, the two janitors, and a couple more guys who jacked fries and flipped burgers at the food court, plus their friends. See, Nicci only made minimum wage at the Corn Dog Dee-Lites stall, and minimum wage was not enough to pay Jenny, her roommate, her cut of the rent, plus food, plus the endless fees, fines, and "re-acclimation"

7

class charges for the DUI that had wrecked her Fusion and separated her from her license. Jenny had been Nicci's best friend since grade school, so splitting an apartment seemed an ideal move to make.

A less-than-ideal move to make was fucking Talbot behind Jenny's back. Talbot was Jenny's fiancé, and he was big, muscular, handsome, and none-too-bright—quite a befitting match for Nicci. His cock couldn't *really* have been the size of a can of tennis balls but it sure *felt* like it. Talbot had a tendency to whisper romantic endearments while he was putting the blocks to her ("Aw, fuck, baby, your pussy's tighter than a bull's ass in fly season" was an example, which Nicci found *very* endearing), and in this selfish, cynical age, romantic endearments were a precious thing indeed, and a welcome verification of love. Plus, Talbot's preposterously large erection made Nicci feel like an overstuffed turkey at Thanksgiving, and, well, she *liked* that feeling. Jenny had no clue what was going on (why should she? Nicci was her best friend! A best friend doesn't fuck your fiancé!) while in the meantime, Nicci upped her oral-sex quotient from one or two per week to five or ten, because poor Talbot only had a part-time job while he was at community college, and with tuition and book costs on a constant rise, he needed help.

On the big day, Nicci had been gargling with Listerine—she always did upon her return from work—when the front door slammed so hard the entire apartment shook.

"That scumbag," came Jenny's whining bellow. "That no good, lying piece of shit!"

Nicci rushed to the kitchen and made the logical enquiry: "Jenny, what's wrong?"

"What's wrong?" Her friend's voice cracked. "I've been giving that muscle-head fiancé of mine $100 a week to help with his college expenses, and you wanna know what I found out today? He's never *been* in college! He never even registered!"

This information didn't sit well with Nicci either, for she'd been giving Talbot the same amount and sometimes more. Therefore, she made the *next* logical enquiry: "If he hasn't been spending the money on college, what *has* he been spending it on?"

"This!" Jenny blurted and slammed something down on the counter. When her hand came away, the material proof of the secret was made plain: a stack of bet cards from the horse track, a *thick* stack, held together with a rubber band, and most for $50 place-and-show bets. All losers.

"Gambling?" Nicci deduced, for perceptivity was not her forte.

"Of course, gambling! And not just horses but greyhounds, roulette, craps, cards, and some shit called harness racing! I found a whole bag of track forms and casino receipts in his apartment. *Now* I know why he never gave me a key!"

"If he never gave you a key, how'd you get in?"

"I *broke* in, and it's a damn good thing I did, 'cos now I know the truth! My fiancé is a *gambling addict!* Of all the lowlife things to be!"

Nicci could think of numerous things more "lowlife" than that: like sucking dick for money, like fucking your best friend's guy. She proverbially shuddered to think what Jenny's reaction might be if she discovered the truth. *But there's no way in hell that could ever happen.* She felt assured. Talbot never pounded her sod in either apartment, only in his car.

"And it gets worse! Look what I found in his car!" And then Jenny pulled something out of her jeans pocket. She held it pinched between thumb and index finger, right in front of Nicci's eyes.

It was a foil packet, about one-and-a-half inches square. It read Lifestyles - Ribbed - Ultra Sensitive - Magnum!

Spittle flew from Jenny's lips. "A fuckin' empty rubber packet!"

Nicci knew what it was—any girl would in this day and age. But the reason a few beads of sweat popped out around her neckline was because Nicci easily recognized the brand. It was one of the packets from the twelve-box she had bought for Talbot.

"That two-timing pile of *fuck* has been fucking someone else behind my back!" Jenny's face, by now, had transformed to the color of a cooked lobster. "When I get my fuckin' hands on that fuckin' slime bucket, I'm gonna fuck him up so fuckin' much he won't know what fuckin' hit him! I'll kick him in the cock *so hard* his dick-knob'll be sticking out his asshole!"

Here was a side of Jenny that Nicci was totally unfamiliar with. Her roommate looked as though the rising pressure of her outrage would cause her face to start percolating. And then, in the space of a blink—

"Oh my God, Nicci, what am I gonna do?" Jenny began to blubber, and then her face fell into her hands and the waterworks began. "I love him so much! Where did I go wrong?"

A situation this complicated left Nicci useless as far as advice and consolation went. All she could think to say was, "There, there, don't worry," and all she could think to do was get a Kleenex as her friend began to hitch, choke, sniffle, and sob unrestrainedly.

But the tissue box on the kitchen counter was empty. *Ah, but I have some in my purse,* she reminded herself, *in one of those little travel packs.* She retrieved her purse opened it, and—

fwap!

The purse had slipped out of her hand and fallen to the floor, and once it hit, a most telling thing was ejected: a veritable ribbon of Lifestyles - Ribbed - Ultra Sensitive - Magnum! condoms.

Jenny's sobs abated rather quickly, for her gaze was at the floor. Then she looked to Nicci, then back to the floor, and then back to Nicci again.

Only the most hackneyed response found its way past Nicci's lips: "Jenny, it's not what you think!"

To make a long story mercifully short, before Jenny kicked Nicci's ass out of the apartment, she just ... kicked Nicci's ass. Her vociferations need not be repeated here, nor do the specific details of the ass-kicking, save to say that her dual black eyes made Nicci appear quite racoonish.

Nicci moved in with Talbot, but this cohabitation was not long-lived. Evidently, his gambling problem was bigger than she could have guessed, and Talbot was eventually found hanging upside-down in an abandoned filling station garage. His impressive genitalia had been cut off with shingle shears, relocated to his mouth, and ramrodded up his throat—yes, *up* his throat instead of *down* his throat because this action had taken place *after* he'd been hung upside-down by a meat hook through his anus—and into his duodenum with a broom handle. She'd heard oblique references to a "big tally" and a "marker" and Talbot "screw-jobbing" a loan shark named "Piccirilli" who worked for a man named "Vinchetti." Nicci could scarcely contemplate these peculiar oddments of the situation; she had more to worry about anyway.

A week later, she was laid off at Corn Dog Dee-Lites, which forced her to escalate her blowjob quotient all the more. Soon, word got around to every oddball who worked at the mall that the "air-head chick who used to work the corn-dog joint does a primo pole-smoke for twenty," and for a short time, Nicci became quite an entrepreneur, until that last oddball turned out to be a US Marshal. She was not surprised that the undercover schmuck had waited until *after* he'd come in her mouth to inform her that she was under arrest.

Unable to make bail, she was sentenced to thirty days in the county detention center, and the experiences she encountered *there*—in what prison parlance dubbed The Lezzie Lounge—are better left to the imagination.

This lengthy narrative, then: to authenticate the sheer *expertise* of Nicci's ability to identifying the taste of semen ...

Her brother, Sam, by the way, happened to be a guard in the same detention facility that had served as Nicci's abode for those thirty punitive days. Sam was an aloof smart-ass, a weirdo and a loner, an inveterate porn-surfer, and, well, a dick, but at least he was decent enough to respect the bond of common blood. After a plethora of snide jokes, he offered his shiftless sister a temporary place to live while she sought new employment.

And now?

Back to the conundrum, that of Nicci's awakening abruptly to find her mouth rife with the taste of sperm. The consideration offered no avenues of question: there was only one person who could've made such a perverse deposit, and worse, now that the bedside light was on, when she looked down at her nude body (Nicci always slept *in statu quo nuditum*), the long lines of pearlescent slime made it clear that Sam had not only ejaculated in her mouth but *all over* her. And, *wow. He comes enough for five guys,* she thought, judging by the sheer *copiousness* of the deposit.

Her fury had her up, out of bed, and hauling on her robe in moments. She thunked barefoot down the hall, bypassing Sam's bedroom (because he slept during the day), and then thunked down the stairs. In the foyer, though, she stopped.

Did she ... *smell* something? Just a trace, but a trace of something *awful.*

She passed it off (*a mouse probably died*) and next was making her way through darkness, down the side hall, to where she *knew* Sam would be: the den, the room where he had his computer and where he often sat for hours scouring porn sites and obligatorily masturbating—she'd heard him in there many times, and had seen the telltale wads of Kleenex in the waste can while cleaning the room. *Guess he decided to jerk off on his sister's face this time, instead of the tissue,* she fumed. She'd caught glimpses of the sites in the past, sites with names like We Are Hairy, Furburger Floozies, Big Bush Bitches (evidently he had a thing for pubic hair), and it came as no surprise when she noticed the line of fluorescent light in the gap under the door.

"I'm really pissed, Sam!" she warned, and banged the door open.

Her brother wasn't there. The lights glared, the computer was on, but no Sam. Fleshy movement on the monitor snagged her eye; ordinarily she wouldn't have cared but—

What on EARTH?

It had been impossible for her not to notice the element of incongruity on the chisel-sharp screen: the image of a bald man inserting his *entire foot* into an obese woman's vaginal vault. Nicci's jaw dropped as she stared. *No, no, no!* she thought for each inch the foot went in. Then the ankle. Then—

"No!"

She scrolled the image away when the first six inches of the man's shin had disappeared into the mammoth crevasse of cookie-dough-white human blubber.

What is *this shit?*

What she'd scrolled to was worse, and worse after that. At the next one, Nicci's stomach did a single hard pump, like a bellows, and she tumbled backward just one pulse away from throwing up. She stumbled more than walked out of the den; so nauseating were the images that she felt dizzy enough to faint. When she'd caught her breath in the dark hallway, her bewilderment socked home. *My brother's worse than a pervert. He's plain and simple* sick in the head! Nicci had heard of off-the-wall porn sites, but this was beyond the pale. On the rare occasions in the past when she'd seen the stuff he was so engrossed in, it was what she could only think of as normal porn, cum-shot compilations, group sex, and an inordinate array of large-busted women displaying abundantly furred pubic plots, but never anything even close to what she'd just seen. Only someone with a serious sexual abnormality would be aroused by such full-tilt misogynistic filth.

A hand landed on her shoulder. "Hey, Sis—"

Nicci shrieked, her heart seeming to stop. The shriek rose and rose, sharpening like a blade, so much that even her own eardrums began to hurt. It was only her brother, of course, returning from the kitchen with a can of soda. When Nicci turned, a hand clenched to her chest, Sam grimaced and ground his teeth at the cacophony.

"*Damn*, Nicci," he bellowed. "Pipe *down!* You're gonna crack all the windows!"

"You scared the ever-loving *fuck* out of me!" she bellowed back.

"Well, what are you doing sneaking around in the middle of the night?"

The shock's adrenalin began to subside, only to be replaced by rage. "I was looking for you, you sick fuck! I saw that twisted shit you were looking at online! You ought to be ashamed of yourself!"

13

Sam's face lengthened in hilarity. "You suck more dicks than a busload of crack whores and *I* should be ashamed?"

"Shut up! You know what I'm talking about!"

"Actually, no, Nicci, I don't. But here's what I *do* know. My sister has had more dicks in her mouth than Charlie Sheen's had champagne. Now *that's* a lot of dicks!" And then he roared laughter.

Nicci *hated* it when he reminded her of how she used to make money. "Fuck you! You're just trying to change the topic—"

"Just how many dicks *did* you suck in your illustrious career? Hundreds? Thousands?"

"Shut up!"

"You know, I'll bet if you measured every dick that's been in your mouth and added them all together, it would be enough to go around the world!"

"Fucker!"

"Twice!"

Now Nicci yelled at a volume that seemed sub-human. "I know what you did upstairs!"

"Did up—"

"And now I know how sick in the head you really are because I just got an eyeful of that disgusting porn you've been looking at! It's *sickening!*"

A puzzled expression came over Sam's face. "Babes with Big Bushes Dot Com? Well, all right, I'm attracted to chicks with pubic hair—none of this clichéd shaved shit, ya know? But what's the big deal with that? You're acting like I was looking at kiddie porn."

"That shit in there is almost as bad!" Nicci continued to yell. "Really, Sam! Japanese girls eating each other's upchuck? Those redneck-looking men making the crippled girl lick a cow's asshole? And then the one with that guy who looks like Elton John pumping turds into a woman's vagina with a fucking *toilet plunger?* I almost threw up!"

"What the hell are you talking about?" He turned, grabbed Nicci's arm, and marched her into the den. "I don't go to sick-pup websites like that. See?"

Sam's mouth fell open when he looked at the screen, where he glimpsed no evidence of Babes with Big Bushes. Instead he saw a fat man blowing his nose into a girl's mouth, after which the girl swallowed, groaned, and opened her mouth for more.

"Fuck!" Sam clicked the website off. "That's not my site—"

"Yeah, right!"

"Nicci. Listen to me. I did *not* go to that website. I don't wanna see sick stuff like that."

She stood hands on hips, tapping a bare foot on the hallway carpet. "Gimme a break. If you didn't go to the site, then who did? The good fucking fairies?"

"It must be a pop-up, you ninny, or one of those viruses that jumps you to other sites. A hopper virus is what they're called."

The remark very quickly tamped down some of Nicci's hostility. "Pop-ups? Viruses?"

"Yeah, pop-ups, viruses. If you had a computer like everyone else in the world, you'd know what I was talking about. Honestly, Nicci, you've sucked so many dicks you must have dick for *brains* now."

Nicci's attitude stalled. She hadn't known that things could change websites like that. But an instant later, the wrath sprang back. "Then what about the cum in my mouth? I can't believe a guy could jerk off in his sister's mouth while she was asleep!"

Sam had been sipping his soda just as Nicci had made this elucidation. He spat the soda all over the wall like the old Johnny Carson Spit Gag.

"Whuh-*what?*" he exclaimed.

"Don't try to lie your way out of it. I know damn well what you did. You got all boned-up looking at that smut, and then you snuck upstairs and beat off in my mouth and all over me. You can't deny it, Sam. There's nobody else in the house. So you damn well better apologize, and while you're at it, get your shit together."

Sam was wiping soda off himself when he replied, "First,

15

let me remind you that I *do* have my shit together. I have a *job.* I have a *car.* I pay the *rent,* I pay the *bills,* and I pay for the *food.* You don't do *shit,* except sit around and watch TV, sleep, and eat the food that *I* pay for—"

"I'm looking for a job!" she countered, but seriously, it was a weak attempt to vindicate herself. The only practical place to work was the mall, and, well, her name was mud there.

"You ain't looked for *dick,*" Sam said, "and speaking of *dick,* the only thing you seem to have any ability to do is—"

"Don't say it!"

"You can't even hold a job selling corn dogs! Only a loser gets fired from a corn-dog stand."

"I didn't get fired! I got let go."

"Yeah, let go, because you were deep-throating every swinging dick in the fuckin' mall." Sam raised a snide finger. "So my point is? *I* have my shit together. *You* don't. And I gotta tell ya, Nicci, you must really have some kind of mental defect to actually think that I would—what?—sneak into your room and jerk off on you?"

"And in my mouth!"

"Right. I didn't know that *sucking dick* killed brain cells, but I guess it fuckin' does."

Nicci had had enough. Sam always did this: threw the mistakes of her past in her face while acting like he was Mr. Responsible. There was only one way to prove her accusation, so …she simply *did* it.

Nicci pulled open her robe and unabashedly exposed her bare breasts, belly, and pubis.

Sam's eyes bugged and he spat more soda onto the wall. "Are you *crazy?* I'm your *brother!* You don't flash your tits and box to your own brother!"

"Yeah? Well just explain this, you fuckin' liar!" Then Nicci drew her finger along the tacky remnants of the sperm that Sam had so bounteously pumped on her.

Only …

"Explain *what?* That your tits are sagging and you're only twenty-five years old?"

The insult didn't register, only the impact of Nicci's befuddlement and even outrage. Not the outrage of being ejaculated on, the outrage of the contradiction: where she *knew* there had been sperm, there was no sperm now. *What the—what the* fuck? Her hands desperately ran up and down her breasts and abdomen, and there was nothing. No moisture, no stickiness, nothing, and when she felt inside her robe for signs of moisture ... nothing. *This is impossible!* In her experience as, well, a head-queen, Nicci had learned a thing or two about, well, cum. It didn't evaporate like water. It didn't just go away. There was always something that remained, a faint, gluey viscosity or a heavy dampness, and if it had dried completely there was *always* the telltale crustiness—which some girls called "leftovers!"—but not here, not now. Nicci's fruitless and embarrassing inspection of herself revealed *no material evidence* of what she *knew* had been all over her only minutes ago. She was as "sperm-free" as if she'd just taken a shower, and—

Come to think of it ...

—that snotty gross-out aftertaste, which always seemed to last for hours, was now nonexistent in her mouth.

Nicci's face turned beet red. She hauled her robe closed. "Holy shit, Sam, it-it-it ... must've been ..."

"Yeah, Einstein, it must've been a dream, and you got no reason calling *me* sick in the head when you're the one who's dreaming about getting a yap-full of her brother's nut. Now go back to bed, ya ditz. And think about looking for a *job* tomorrow."

Nicci's eyes fluttered. "Sam, I'm sorry. I don't know what to say. It's just that I could've sworn—"

"Go back to bed!"

And that Nicci did, more confused than she could ever remember being.

But the next night was worse. Nicci lay naked atop the mattress, asleep but shuddering. Part of her consciousness felt tethered to her, but as hard as she tried, she could not wake up or open her eyes or make even direct movement of her arms

17

and legs. And along with this black paralysis came a notion that was impossible to dispel: that she was not alone in the room.

She sensed someone standing at the bedside looking down. The "someone" had to be Sam, it *had* to be, because even in her distressed slumber, Nicci knew there was no one else in the house. She tried to reach up and to the right, to touch him, to feel some evidence of his physical presence and therefore validate that she was not really dreaming, but her arm lay still like a dummy's limb. Only her fingers twitched.

She smelled something awful. It was a faint smell but so indescribably appalling that her stomach muscles began to heave, and as something rushed up, she knew she was about to vomit.

Instead ...

Something hit her in the face like a bucket of hot, chunky soup, and at once it was not Nicci who was vomiting, it was someone else. Vomiting, yes, right in her face, and with such force and volume she knew now that this *had* to be a dream, a *nightmare,* because no one could throw up *this much.* The previous faint odor was now replaced by a stench that had to be worse than excrement, urine, pus-stained bandages, and the effluence at the bottom of a meat-market dumpster on the hottest day of summer, all mixed up together in one big goulash of horror. Oatmeal from hell might be one allusion to draw. The expulsion was accompanied by a mine-shaft-deep basso warble akin to, "*Arg-a-lar-gur-lar-gur-larrrrrrrr ...*" amid an under-sound like wet concrete pouring. Nicci convulsed in the abominable inundation, one gust, two, three, and a fourth as long as the first three combined.

Heaving breath, she spat out that which had entered her mouth and was then vomiting herself, only to realize that her hips were bucking like electrodes attached to a frog's legs and the reason for the bucking was due to some organic object wriggling abruptly up and into her vagina. When she tried to open her eyes she was unable, and likewise she found herself absolutely incapable of screaming, for she knew now beyond all reckoning that none of this could be sloughed off as mere dream. And she knew this too: *Someone's putting his hand all the way up my pussy, and it's* not *Sam!*

It couldn't be, for Sam didn't have hands more than a foot long, and they weren't bump-covered, and they weren't slimy. And all the way up this impossible hand went until she felt seemingly joint-less fingers frolicking in her reproductive canal. Then—

Shhhhhhhhhhhh-ULP!

—the "hand" was withdrawn, like a boot pulled out of mud. Just as inexplicably as everything else was that this horrific violation of her privates left her … *stimulated.* She felt her sex juicing. She felt her nipples harden. And most outrageous of all was Nicci's next observation, that she wanted that stimulation repeated. She still could not move or open her eyes but at last she was able to croak out a few words.

"Pluh-please, do it again! Stick it in again!"

Nicci's request would not be honored. What she got instead was—

"*Arg-a-lar-gur-lar-gur-larrrrrrr—*"

—more vomit.

But not in her face this time. This time—

Holy fuck—no!

—directly into her mouth. What must have been its left hand pushed down on her forehead, and what must have been the right pushed down on her chin. Thus, the latter gesture cranked her mouth open, which, in her paresis, she could not in a million years close. Even in the madness, in the sheer impossible consternation, Nicci supposed she knew what was coming next:

Lips like an open wound sealed against her mouth and—

"*Arg-a-lar-gur-lar-gur-larrrrrrrr!*"

—this burglar, this person, this thing—whatever it was— wasted no time introducing the "oatmeal from hell" into her mouth. It was *so much* that Nicci grimly realized that as the vomit was forced down her throat, she would surely choke to death on it, which left her two choices. One, she could do just that, drown in vomit and kiss the world good-bye, or two—

Gotta swallow …

Indeed, there was only one way to evacuate all that vomit, and that was to ingest it, and ingest it Nicci did, cleverly timing her technique. When one gust blew into her mouth, she paused, swallowed, and then prepared for the next. The lip-lock maintained itself through more than a couple of gusts, and when it was over, Nicci lay twitching on the bed like in the throes of a mild electrocution, and now she sported a little potbelly from all she'd swallowed.

Schlucking sounds signaled the trespasser's departure, and a second later, Nicci could open her eyes and move. Her molester's exit switched off the paralysis. Hot, reeking vomit slid lava-like down her chest when she leaned up, gagging and dizzy from the sensation of all that upchuck sloshing around in her belly. The chunks and particles seemed to locomote with deliberateness, as if each piece possessed a motility of its own. Most of her power of reason, and her power of speculation, was kept far away from her volition. She knew only one thing: *I will prove this to Sam! I will show him I'm not crazy and I'm not dreaming!* How could he deny it when he saw the evidence for himself? What could he say? That the blanket of evil-smelling puke was her imagination?

Yeah, I'll show that smart-ass fucker!

Nicci then rushed out of the bedroom and down the stairs, belly sloshing and vomit pouring off her. "Sam! Come out! I just got thrown up on!"

Her progress ushered her down, down the dim hall at whose end she saw the light beneath the door. "Sam! Forget about your fuckin' porn and come *out* here!"

THUMP!

In the next instant, Nicci's butt was on the floor. She'd fallen hard, and it seemed that she'd stepped on something she hadn't noticed. She'd slipped, and it felt like something slick and mushy that she'd slipped on, like a banana peel. Nearly senseless now, she kneed herself forward, leaned, and pushed open the door to the den. This action threw an ample wedge of bright fluorescent light across half the hallway, and she beheld the object on which she'd slipped and fallen. It was no banana peel; instead, it was a penis and a pair of testicles in a scrotum, not cut but torqued off the victim's groin.

The victim, of course, was Sam, and it was at this point that Nicci lost consciousness, never noticing that the blanket of vomit that had covered her none too long ago was now completely gone, and gone too was the potbelly caused by ingestion of said vomit.

The police would find the rest of Sam all over the house: his face, scalp, and ears in the den; hands and feet in the living room; and the rest in varying stages of separation in other places. Exactly where hardly mattered. The county medical examiner, however, would cite that the victim had been "physically dismantled via a mode of incalculable violence, the nature of which I am as yet unable to determine."

Preposterously, Nicci was suspected with more than a small amount of judicial vigor, but she was never charged due to her passing of a battery of polygraphs, an MRI lie-detection test, and several psychiatric evaluations. When asked if she had murdered her brother, her answer of "No" registered as truth on the machine, and when asked if she knew who did, a same result registered by her answer of, "I'm not sure, but I think it was a monster." She was then determined to be incompetent to stand trial and next became a guest of the state department of mental health's "locked dormitory unit."

So that was it for Nicci.

And what of the house at Sixty-Five Stirrup Iron Road, in which all this mayhem had occurred?

It would not be inhabited again until—

CHAPTER ONE
EDWARD LEE
AND J. F. GONZALEZ

Ten Years Later

Arrianne looked faintly awestruck out the back window. She could see the centuried trees, the quaint stone fence lining the road that marked the yard's end, and the sloping grasslands beyond. Birds frolicked as they hunted for worms, butterflies gently roved, and a young deer meandered along the fence. And at the bottom of the grassland's decline: the lake.

The scene was idyllic, and Arrianne realized she'd never felt more content in her life. *I'm so glad Chuck found this wonderful house and property,* she told herself. *The city was starting to make me feel ancient, but now ...*

She felt wonderful.

So wonderful, in fact, that an undeniable arousal began to tingle through her bosom, down her belly, and to her—

The door clunked open, and in walked her husband, a big carryout bag from Leroy Selman's under one arm and something else under the other, a long box printed with the words Keene Industries, LTD.

"Let me help," she said and rushed over.

"I got it," Chuck said. On his face was that almost constant look of self-satisfaction.

She always joked that he looked like Mitt Romney. "Thanks," he said once, "and I may *look* like him, but I feel about as old as his father," this being part of the way they both jested about getting older, and the settling of the years upon them, and how it seemed to happen without their ever realizing it.

She took the carry-out bag and put it on the counter. The intoxicating aroma of smoked ribs filled the kitchen.

"I know how you love Selman's ribs," he said, and then

set the much-heavier parcel on the counter as well.

"Yes, I do, but I guess you *don't* know how hard I've been trying to diet."

"Diet-schmiet. It's Saturday."

Arrianne gently laughed at the dismissal. *Oh, well. I guess I can restart the diet tomorrow.* She changed the subject to get her mind off the food. "Did you get the traps?"

"Sure did," he said. He placed down a smaller bag he'd brought in. "Got four of them."

"The kind that doesn't kill them, right?"

"Of course! What do I look like? Vlad the Impaler of Rodents?"

This relieved Arrianne, a lifelong animal lover. Rats, sure, but mice and chipmunks? She couldn't abide the thought of using poison or the typical spring-traps that killed them, so Chuck agreed to buy humane traps, the kind that seized the animals alive, and then they could be let go somewhere far away from the house. Winter was coming, and half the rooms in the house weren't getting heat. They'd actually seen the chipmunks venturing out at night, and during the day they heard them scampering back and forth in the overhead ducts.

"I was talking to the guy at Home Depot," Chuck told her—now he was opening the big box. "He said trapping them won't solve the problem. It's not the chipmunks themselves that are blocking the airflow, it's their nesting material."

Arrianne paused on the remark. "That never occurred to me. Guess we'll have to get a heating and air-conditioning technician to get rid of the nests, huh?"

"That would cost a fortune, and you know how those shylocks are. Probably charges $75 an hour and you can bet he'll take his sweet time finding the nests. So ... I figure we can cut that service fee way down by locating the nests ourselves."

Arrianne looked puzzled. "How do we do that?"

"We do it ... with this!" and by then, Chuck had opened the box. "A Keene Model 4A Boroscopic Conduit Inspection System, also known as a video snake!"

Arrianne looked at the contraption Chuck had pulled out of the box with a sense of wonder. In a way it looked like a taser gun with a long black cable that came out of what should be the barrel. On what would have been the rear of the unit was a video screen just above the grip. Chuck held the thing, grinning like a little kid.

"You feed this in the air ducts," he said, his left hand moving along the black cable, "and you can see what's up there with the screen. The cable has a fifteen-foot reach."

"And if you find the ducts blocked with a nest, how do you get it out?"

"Easy. With this!" Chuck reached into the box and pulled out another contraption. This one Arrianne recognized. It was what plumbers call a snake.

"You're gonna use a plumber's snake to remove chipmunk nests from the air ducts?"

"Sure. One of us can use the Boroscope to keep our sight on it while the other cleans the nest out with the snake."

Arrianne couldn't help but voice her next concern. "What if there's chipmunk babies in there? Won't this kill them?"

"What else can we do?"

Arrianne didn't have an answer for that. She picked up the bag from Selman's and took it to the kitchen. She began to get plates out of the cupboard as Chuck placed the snake and the Boroscope back in the box.

"Look, I know how you feel about animals," Chuck began. "We'll be really careful about this, I promise."

Arrianne began dishing up plates for their dinner. The ribs smelled wonderful. She sighed, looking over at Chuck. "I know, and I appreciate your concern, but …"

"I know it's been a while," Chuck said. He approached the kitchen's island where Arrianne was getting their plates together—Chuck had picked up smoked ribs, coleslaw, baked potatoes, and macaroni and cheese. "And I know that what happened to Teddy was terrible, but—"

"I don't want to talk about it," Arrianne said.

Chuck stopped. He looked uncomfortable. "I'm sorry. It's just that …"

Arrianne finished dishing out the plates. She looked at him, trying to contain her emotions. She took a deep breath. "I know it's been hard, but really, I'm doing better."

"Are you? Really?"

"Yes." She nodded and went to the refrigerator. She pulled out a carafe of water and then pulled down two glasses from the cupboard. "Chipmunks are just a fact of life. They're not rats. What happened to Teddy ... well, we *know* what happened. This isn't the same thing."

"Of course," Chuck said. Arrianne poured them each a glass of water. With their plates in hand, they headed to the dining room and sat at the table.

They took their meal in silence for a while, savoring the ribs, which was a specialty at Selman's. Now that the subject of Teddy had come up again, Arrianne couldn't get him out of her mind.

Teddy had been their cat at their previous home. A male calico. He'd been neutered, but it hadn't stopped him from wandering their old neighborhood. Because he was neutered, he wasn't as territorial as un-neutered males, and he didn't wander far. However, he did have a strong prey drive. Birds, mice ...

If it was a critter, Teddy would hunt it down, kill it, and bring the remains right to their doorstep.

Arrianne had seen it plenty of times. Birds, chipmunks, frogs. Teddy would leave their mutilated remains on the front porch of their Brooklyn duplex as if it was an offering. A few times Teddy had brought lizards and garter snakes, a few times he'd even brought a squirrel or two.

She'd never seen Teddy bring home a rat.

Arrianne had found him when she'd exited the garage after coming home from work. Teddy had managed to crawl back to the garage and had been lying on his side near the door that led to the backyard. She'd given a startled yelp and dropped her purse. Teddy had laid there on his side, his fur matted with dried blood, his left eye gouged out and hanging out of its socket. He'd been panting heavily. Arrianne had quickly composed herself and knelt down, trying to keep her panic down as she visually assessed Teddy. He looked pretty torn up, but he was alive. Had he been in a fight with another cat? That was her first thought as she'd bundled him up in her coat, put him in the front seat of the car, and headed to the vet.

Their vet, Dr. Ketchum, had been unable to save Teddy. It was primarily the shock that did him in. Teddy died in one of Dr. Ketchum's examination rooms as he and a vet assistant worked at stabilizing him.

Later it was determined that Teddy had suffered multiple puncture wounds that looked to be caused by long incisors, like those from a rat. Multiple scratches along Teddy's belly and flank looked to be from claws. A tuft of skin and fur recovered from Teddy's paws was conclusive.

"Hard to believe, but your cat was killed by a rat," Dr. Ketchum told her a few days later when she'd stopped by the vet's office to collect Teddy's ashes. "I know you've heard that New York rats are a breed of their own—the ones in the subways are thought to be descendants of Norway rats that came aboard freighter ships. My guess is Teddy came across a mother rat with a nest of babies. A mother rat won't give a damn how big you are. I've heard of them attacking people."

Arrianne didn't even know there was a family of rats near the house, but a few days later she found it—somehow, the bugger had built a nest beneath one of the rain gutters along the side of the house. Tufts of cat hair were scattered over an area near some bushes amid spatters of blood, evidence from Teddy's fatal altercation. She took a step forward for a better look and was instantly charged by the varmint, who came dashing out its burrow. Arrianne had been quick on her heels and scampered back. The goddamn thing chased her nearly all the way to the garage. It had stood in the middle of the yard, chattering at her, yelling at her, it seemed, and then had darted back into the bushes that hid its underground nest.

Chuck had offered to call an exterminator, but she'd discouraged that. If it was a rat that had a litter she was only doing what any mother would do—protect its babies. Sure enough, as the weeks passed, she'd started to see the babies as they crept out of the nest their mama rat had made for them— and mama rat was pretty goddamn big, as she observed one night from the second-story bedroom window, looking down at their yard as the mother rat sat perched on top of their garbage can, rummaging for food. And while part of her had considered revenge, had wanted to take Chuck up on his offer to have the goddamn thing killed, she couldn't bring herself to go through with it. What had happened had just been an unfortunate series of events. Teddy had paid for it with his life.

"Maybe once we take care of whatever it is that's making that noise in our attic, we should think about an addition to our household," Chuck said, breaking the silence.

Arrianne looked up from her meal. She was almost finished. "Another cat? I don't know ..."

"I wasn't thinking about another cat. I was thinking a dog."

"A dog? I don't know ..."

"I know you're not a dog person. Especially those little yappy kinds."

Arrianne shrugged. She picked at her coleslaw. "Why a dog?"

"Well, it would have to be a non-terrier type dog," he said. "Terriers were bred to hunt rats and squirrels, so rodents would drive any kind of terrier crazy. I was thinking more of a shepherd, or maybe a golden retriever."

A golden? Arrianne turned the thought over. When she was a kid, her family had had a golden retriever.

"Either a golden or a shepherd. Maybe an Australian shepherd."

Arrianne finished her meal, thinking about what Chuck had suggested. A cat might not be in the cards, especially in such a rural area where she'd be freaked out all the time, reliving the incident with Teddy over and over. But a dog ...

She looked up at Chuck as he stood up and removed his dish and glass from the table and walked over to the kitchen. "I like that idea," she said.

Chuck stopped, looked back at her. "Really?"

"Really."

Chuck smiled.

CHAPTER TWO
J. F. GONZALEZ

After a leisurely breakfast of cut fruit and coffee, where they spent most of the morning on the back deck passing various sections of the Sunday paper back and forth, Chuck headed upstairs to shower and get dressed while Arrianne cleaned up the breakfast dishes. As she stacked the dishwasher, Arrianne thought about what they'd talked about last night. Maybe a dog would be just the thing they needed to brighten things up around here. They'd made this move to the country as a last-ditch effort to save their marriage and their sanity. Teddy's death had been the catalyst that had brought Arrianne's depression back full force. Therapy didn't even help this time, and when she began to entertain thoughts of driving her car into an interstate embankment or off a bridge, she realized she needed help. A visit with a psychiatrist had resulted in a prescription for Lexapro and more intensive therapy. After that she began to stabilize. And with that came the suggestion that they vacate the duplex in Brooklyn for new digs in a more rural, more suburban environment.

As she stacked the dishwasher and cleaned up the kitchen, Arrianne thought about the last five months. Things had happened so quickly—the attack on Teddy, her worsening depression, Chuck losing his consulting job, and Arrianne's own job woes. All this had contributed to a strain in their marriage, and when her psychiatrist, Dr. White, suggested that moving to a different location might help in the recovery process, Chuck had taken it upon himself to get the ball rolling. By then Chuck had bounced back with another consulting assignment—this time working remotely for a client located in Wisconsin. His new schedule allowed him to look around for a house, and he quickly found this place— Sixty-Five Stirrup Iron Road.

When he'd shown her the listing, she'd thought it was too good to be true. "What's wrong with it?" she remembered asking when he passed the flyer to her. It had contained photos and all the information on the house. "This place looks beautiful, it's in a great location, and it's just what we need, but the price ... my God, Chuck, it's a *steal!* What's wrong with it?"

There was nothing wrong with it, at least not on the surface. The home inspection had returned no defects. The only thing Chuck had been able to get out of the seller was that the home was being sold by an estate. Perhaps the former owner had died in it? The seller denied this was the case—they'd never lived in the house, had only used it as rental property. Everything about the house had screamed *this is a great deal! Buy now!*

So he'd made an offer that was accepted.

They'd moved in a month ago and were now pretty firmly settled. Chuck was now working remotely from home on a new consulting assignment as a technical writer, while Arrianne had managed to turn her existing position as a contract specialist into a telecommuting position. Their work schedules were in perfect synch with each other, and the change in location was so far working wonders on her emotional well-being.

And for once, their sex life was improving.

Arrianne thought back to last night as she closed the dishwasher. During the depths of her depression, she'd been uninterested in sex. Chuck had taken it like a trooper and given her space and time. But since moving into this home, Arrianne had found her sexual desires awakening. And with it came new desires and a need to push the envelope past her comfort zone. Chuck had been pleasantly surprised. Especially last night.

"What's gotten into you?" Chuck gasped when their coupling last night was finished. He panted, his chest and face slick with sweat. "You've ... you've never ..."

"Wanted you in my ass before?" Arrianne had asked, moving her leg over his, nuzzling him. She'd gripped his penis, still lubricated with their juices. "Well, since moving here, that's all changed."

29

"You can say that again."

Arrianne stepped into the living room. From the back of the house, toward the master bedroom and bath, she heard the shower start up. She smiled. She felt a tingling in her breasts, in her loins. Chuck surely wouldn't mind if she joined him in the shower. Besides, she needed one too.

She was right. He didn't mind.

They spent the rest of the day using the Boroscope to see if chipmunks had, indeed, built nests in the air ducts in the home's heating and cooling system. They explored all areas of the system with the Boroscope, and all corners of it showed no signs that the house was infested with chipmunks or their nests.

That left the attic. They ventured up later that afternoon and explored it thoroughly. No chipmunks, squirrels, or mice had taken up residence—there were no shredded bits of newspaper and debris that would indicate nests, no mounds of sawdust indicating termites, no droppings. In short, the attic was completely bare. Dusty but bare.

From beginning to end it took them two hours to do a complete search of the house and investigate the air conditioning and heating ducts with the Boroscope. They also conducted a physical search of the home and the basement.

Chuck looked a little puzzled. "We've seen the chipmunks outside, right? I mean, we hear the noises and then later see them moving away from the house, as if they're leaving from wherever it is they've holed themselves into. But there's no evidence they've built nests anywhere in the house. Something's got to be making that noise."

"Maybe it's just our imagination," Arrianne had said. "Let's forget about it for now and clean up. Maybe we can get an early dinner in town?"

That lifted Chuck's spirits and they'd retired to the master bedroom/bathroom where they showered again. And showering led to another round of sex, this time starting on the bathroom floor and ending up in the bedroom. Arrianne had gobbled his cock hungrily as she fingered herself and when Chuck exploded in her face, she'd licked every drop, smearing his ejaculate around her lips and licking it off her fingers. It was a perfect way to end their chores for the day.

They'd turned in early that evening because Chuck had to rise early for a conference call. As they lay in bed, drifting off to sleep, a scuttling sound in the attic perked Arrianne. She nudged Chuck with her elbow. "You hear that?"

"What?" Chuck rolled over, frowning.

"Listen!"

They remained still and silent. The scuttling sound came again, like pattering feet scampering back and forth above their heads in the attic.

"They've got to be getting in somewhere we missed," Chuck said, throwing the covers off and getting out of bed.

Arrianne got out of bed and pulled on her robe. She followed Chuck as he pulled the collapsible ladder down from the attic, and armed with a flashlight, he began to head up. Arrianne was right behind him, eager to see what was up there.

Nothing was in the attic.

"I heard it," Chuck said, his hair sticking up from his head. He looked completely confused in the light from the flash. "It sounded like—"

"Something running around up here," Arrianne finished.

"Could it have been the tree branches rubbing against the side of the house?" Chuck turned to the north side of the house. "It *is* kinda windy, and that elm's branches are right up against the eaves on this side."

Arrianne didn't know what to make of that. She supposed it was possible, but no, she'd heard it as clear as day. What she'd heard was the pitter-patter of feet racing across the ceiling, running from one end of the attic to the other.

"Something else I noticed," Chuck said as they climbed down and he folded the ladder back up. "Do you smell anything funny?"

"Smell anything funny? Like what?"

Chuck closed the door to the attic and shrugged. "Best way I can describe it is it smells like something crawled in the eaves or the walls of the house and died."

31

Arrianne sniffed the air and shook her head. "I don't smell anything."

Chuck looked puzzled. "That's weird. I can smell it very faintly. I noticed it last week too."

"Last week?"

"Yeah." They headed back to the master bedroom and got back into bed. "And I thought I smelled it a week or two after we moved in, and then it was gone."

"But now you smell it again?"

Chuck sat up in bed and sniffed the air again. "I don't smell it from here. I definitely smelled it out in the hall."

"Well, I didn't smell anything in the hall." Arrianne settled back in bed and drew the covers over her. "I'm tired. Let's get some sleep."

The following day was Monday, a workday. The windstorm from last night had died down, and right before lunch Arrianne had taken the trash out. When she entered the kitchen, Chuck was getting a midday snack.

"Maybe we should get an exterminator," she suggested. "Seventy-five bucks will buy us expertise and peace of mind."

Chuck nodded. He sighed. "I'll call when I get back from my business trip on Thursday."

"There was nothing disclosed on the seller's info that the house had a pest problem?"

"Nope."

"They had to have the same kind of experience. Even though the chipmunks or mice or whatever it is they are haven't invaded the house, the former owners probably had tenants that experienced what we're going through. I wonder what they did to deal with the problem."

"I don't know, and we can't find out," Chuck said. He took an apple out of the fruit bowl and began to head back to his office. He glanced at Arrianne. "We can't exactly contact the tenants who lived here."

Arrianne shook her head.

"We'll figure this out. I'll call an exterminator when I get back."

"Maybe if I finish early today, I'll look for one," Arrianne said.

"You do that."

Arrianne frowned as Chuck headed back to his office. She got the impression Chuck was avoiding something. But what? The conversation sent Arrianne back into old habits. She shut down. Retreated. Burying herself in work had always done wonders in the past. Today was no exception. She headed back to her office, which was next to Chuck's, and tried to get back into work, to avoid thinking about it. Within time, she did.

She treaded lightly around the subject that evening during dinner, hoping to elicit a response from Chuck. He merely repeated the same thing he'd said that morning, that he didn't know what was causing the sound and that securing the services of a professional exterminator was the best course of action. He was right, of course.

After the dinner dishes were stowed in the dishwasher and the evening chores were done, they sat on their respective ends of the sofa. The plasma-screen TV was on. Arrianne was flipping through the channels. Chuck was flipping through the latest issue of *Esquire*.

"Were you serious about wanting to get a dog?"

Chuck looked up from the article he was reading. "Of course."

"You want to maybe pay a visit to the local shelter this weekend, after you get back from your trip?"

"Absolutely."

"Good." Arrianne smiled at him. Chuck smiled back. All was right in the world. Once again, they were in synch. A dog would help bring things in balance. And a dog would keep her company for those days when Chuck was out traveling on business.

They watched two programs that had been DVRd last night—*The Walking Dead* and *Dexter*—and then went to bed. Chuck fell asleep immediately. Arrianne lay on her side, her body tired but her mind racing with a thousand thoughts.

33

After a while, she dozed.

But she couldn't fall asleep completely. She felt a stirring of desire between her thighs, a tingle in her breasts. She turned toward Chuck. He was in a deep sleep, lying on his right side, his back to her. No way was he coming out of it. Trying to rouse Chuck out of a deep sleep was like trying to resurrect the dead—it just didn't happen. Frustrated and horny, Arrianne turned on her left side and her right hand darted between her legs. She rubbed her sex, letting her fingers slip inside her. That calmed the urge down and the feeling faded for some reason. She frowned. That was weird. It was as if all the desire, all the horniness she'd felt had gone away.

Now she was completely awake. She got out of bed, slipped on her robe, and exited the bedroom.

She headed down the hallway and paused in the doorway of Chuck's office—the light from his computer screen was illuminating the hallway.

The screensaver on Chuck's computer was not on, nor had the computer gone to sleep, which was what he had it set to do after one hour of inactivity. Instead, the screen was active, as if it was being used.

A pornography website was on the screen.

What the ...?

Arrianne stepped into Chuck's office, and her revulsion hit the stratosphere.

On the screen, a fat homeless-looking guy was giving it to a dumpy-looking woman doggie-style. They were in what appeared to be an abandoned building; the floor was littered with trash, and there was graffiti on the walls. They were fucking on a very worn, very dirty mattress. The homeless-looking guy had no teeth; the woman had very greasy hair and looked dirty. Just as he reached his climax, he pulled out. Only instead of the requisite money shot, fatso maneuvered himself over toward the woman's face as she simultaneously switched positions, lying on her back. Fatso wasn't even stroking his puny dick at this point. Instead, he leaned over the woman ...

"Arg-a-lar-gur-lar-gur-larrrrrrrr—"

... and unleashed a stream of vomit on her face.

"What the *fuck*!" Arrianne said.

The vomit hit the woman's face in a clumpy mess; it looked like chunks of soup and gravy all mixed together. The woman was making moaning sounds, as if she were enjoying it. She was masturbating with one hand and smearing the vomit around her face and shoving chunks into her mouth with the other. Fatso had only vomited one great upheaval of stomach contents. He gagged, appeared as if he were going to vomit again, and then seemed to catch his breath. As if realizing his nausea had passed, he resumed stroking himself again. His pudgy fist whipped his skinny little dick. Fascinated, Arrianne could only stand there in numb silence as fatso ejaculated, spattering spurts of milky semen on the woman's face. The woman mixed it in with the vomit, licking her vomit- and semen-encrusted fingers.

"*Chuck!*" Arrianne yelled. This was really fucked up, and they were going to have words about this. Now.

"Chuck, get your ass in here. *Now!*"

No response from Chuck. He was zonked out.

As quickly as her anger and disgust hit her, it was starting to dissipate. Okay, fine. She'd talk to him about this tomorrow before he left. She knew Chuck had looked at online pornography before—what man hadn't?—but this was just crossing the line. Why the fuck would anyone want to watch videos of homeless people throwing up on each other? Was this how Chuck felt about women? While she knew intellectually and personally that the answer was no—she knew Chuck too well, and he was not like that—part of her wondered if she hadn't stumbled on some dark and dirty secret he kept under lock and key. She wondered if he'd forgotten to close the web browser when he was finished with work. It would be just like him. The bastard.

Arrianne stepped up to the computer, and grabbing the mouse, she clicked out of the browser just as another video started. She clicked out of a few pop-up ads that had appeared on the screen ("One woman, five dicks!" "Dumpster sluts!" "Monkey Love!"). Then she put the computer to sleep and exited Chuck's office. There was no way she was getting to sleep now, and even if she got tired she didn't think she could go back to bed. It looked like she'd be sleeping on the couch tonight.

Which was what she did. Arrianne positioned herself on her end of the couch, and feet up, she flipped through the channels on the TV to find something to cleanse her mind of what she'd seen. She found an old movie on Turner Classics—Hitchcock's *North by Northwest*—and settled into it. An hour later, she began to feel drowsy. She flicked the TV off with the remote control, and right before she fell asleep she thought she detected the faint odor of something rotten, something so foul that at first she thought it was part of a dream.

CHAPTER THREE
J. F. GONZALEZ
AND BRIAN KEENE

Arrianne had coffee going and had almost finished her first cup when Chuck entered the kitchen. He was already showered and dressed and ready for his business trip. He headed straight for the coffee pot, grabbed a mug from the cupboard, and poured himself a cup.

"Did you sleep on the sofa last night?"

"Yeah, I did." Arrianne finished her coffee and glared at him from the breakfast nook. "Guess what I found on your computer?"

"My computer?" Chuck looked puzzled as he turned to her, but when he saw the expression on her face, his puzzlement turned to concern. "What? What happened?"

"Guys throwing up on women? Really, Chuck?"

"What are you talking about?"

"You were surfing porn yesterday afternoon before you closed out of work for the day, weren't you?"

"No!"

"Really?"

"Yes, really." Chuck's denial had been automatic and genuinely assertive. She knew instantly he was telling the truth. "I was too goddamn busy to surf for porn. What the fuck, Arrianne!" Chuck looked at her as if she'd lost her mind.

"So you don't deny that you've ever surfed for porn on your work computer?"

"What is this about?"

"Just answer the question! Have you ever searched for porn on your computer in your office?"

There was a slight hesitation, and then he said, "Yes, I have. And so what? I get curious, and I do a little trolling for smut. What guy doesn't?"

"And you didn't search for any yesterday?"

"No, I did not."

Hard as it was for Arrianne to admit, she believed him. Part of her wanted to be angry at him, but she just couldn't do it. She knew Chuck too well. Knew what turned him on and what turned him off. And she knew he simply would not have been into watching people throw up on each other during sex. That was as bad as being shit on or pissed on. Only sick fucks did that. The furthest they'd ever gone, prior to Arrianne letting Chuck take her up the ass, was some light bondage. Harmless stuff. No humiliation at all.

"When was the last time you surfed for porn on your computer?"

Chuck shrugged. "I don't know. A few months?"

"It didn't seem that way last night," Arrianne said. She suddenly felt cold and drew the robe tighter over her breasts. "The stuff I saw on your computer … it was *sick*."

Chuck set the coffee cup down and headed toward his office. Arrianne debated following him and then got off the stool and tailed him.

She got to his office just as he reached his desk. He woke his computer up and stared at it for a moment. The computer looked normal. On the screen was his normal backdrop—a desert scene from their vacation at the Grand Canyon last year.

Chuck turned to her. "What did you see?"

"It was sick. This fat guy, he looked like a homeless guy, was fucking this chick, and instead of pulling out and coming all over her, he just … he threw up on her."

"He threw up on her?"

"Yeah." Arrianne felt embarrassed now. "I know it sounds weird, Chuck, but I swear—"

Chuck opened a web browser. The Google home page came up. He clicked on history and scrolled down to the day before. And there it was:

SKIDROW SEXCAPADES!

"What the hell is this?" Chuck clicked on the page, and when it came up Arrianne saw the same layout she'd seen the night before, all high-end graphics rendered in florescent blue and red with blinking animated gifs. In the center of the page a video started up. This time, the scene was an alley of some inner city. A woman with heroin-sculpted cheeks was on her knees in front of an emaciated guy with pus-laden scabs running up his arms, blowing him. They both looked like they'd been living on the streets for years. Even their dirt had dirt on it.

Chuck pulled up the history tab again and, ignoring the slurping, sucking sounds coming from the computer, noted the date stamp on yesterday's time slot. "What time did you see this?"

Arrianne shrugged. "Around one in the morning."

"The time stamp on this is twelve thirty." He scrolled through the previous site— Diseased Whores and Suppurating Dicks. The time stamp on that was shortly before midnight. They'd gone to bed last night around ten thirty. Chuck clicked out of the web browser. "I don't know what the hell is going on here, but I didn't access that site. You saw the time stamp." He looked at Arrianne, his features grim.

"Okay, okay, I'm sorry," Arrianne said. She felt at a loss. "How the hell did this happen?"

"I don't know." Chuck clicked around various folders, opened files, read things. "I'd hate to think a hacker got in. I don't have file sharing turned on, and I don't have time to look through my logs to see what kind of network activity was going on at that time."

"Maybe ..."

Chuck pushed away from the computer and stood up. "Listen, I'm sorry I got mad at you, but you see this wasn't me that was surfing those sites last night, right?"

Arrianne nodded.

"I've really got to get out the door and to my meeting, and I have a three-hour drive. Call your IT people and have them do a check on your system and our home network. Ask them to look at the time period between eleven last night and two in the morning. If somebody outside our network hacked in, they did it when we were asleep, and they breached our firewall and gained remote access to my computer. Speaking of which ..." Chuck reached over to his mouse and shut down his computer.

As the computer shut down, Chuck looked more relaxed. "Tell them there was an intrusion attempt on my computer last night. They'll run tests and probably run an anti-Trojan horse program on your computer to see if somebody tried to gain access to it. When I get home, I'll run a more thorough scan on my computer."

"Okay." She nodded, pouting. Her lower lip quivered with emotion, her embarrassment and frustration evident.

"Hey …" Chuck rose from the chair and crossed over to her. Then he took Arrianne in his arms and pulled her close. "It's okay. I'm not angry. I would have probably freaked out too, if I'd seen that crap on your computer."

She nodded again, into his neck. Chuck held her closer. Arrianne's nipples stiffened as she felt his breath on her skin. She let her hands slide down his body, her fingers gliding over his muscles.

"Hey, now." Smiling, Chuck gently pushed her away. "I've got to go. I'm late! We'll pick this up when I get home Thursday night, okay?"

"That sounds good." Arrianne returned his smile, trying not to let her disappointment show. "Call me when you get to the hotel, and let me know you made it safe."

"Will do." He kissed her forehead. "I love you."

"I love you too. Be careful."

"I will. You too."

Arrianne stood in the bay window, watching him leave. Perspiration formed on her upper lip. Her breathing grew heavy and her legs trembled. She waited until his car had left the driveway and passed from sight before rushing to the couch and masturbating until she'd received two orgasms in quick succession. When the frenzy was over, she was covered in sweat and deliciously exhausted—but also a little disturbed. Her libido had never been this demanding, this *frantic* before. There had to be an explanation for this seemingly sudden change, but what could it be? Could it have something to do with their marriage? Arrianne had heard about all the various hills and valleys a married couple's sex life went through, but this didn't seem like that. She wondered if it could be a hormonal issue. Surely she was too young for any premenopausal symptoms. Wasn't she? Arrianne frowned. Maybe she was ovulating. She considered the possibility but decided it didn't make much sense. She ovulated every month after all, but it had never left her this horny before.

Still frowning and pondering, she got up from the couch and headed for the shower. As she walked, she ran through a mental checklist of tasks for the day. Arrianne had always found that when she was feeling stressed or overwhelmed or confused, it helped her to make lists and check things off them.

"I have to remember to call the IT guys when I'm done," she said aloud.

But there was something else that Arrianne hadn't remembered. She'd been so intent on satisfying her carnal needs, she had neglected to lock the front door after Chuck had departed.

CHAPTER FOUR
BRIAN KEENE

Zito drove slowly past the house on Stirrup Iron Road two more times in his red Ford pickup, trying to decide if what he was contemplating was worth the risk—and if he really had the stomach to go through with it. He also wondered what would happen if it all went wrong, and just where in the blue fuck this crazy idea had come from in the first place.

Originally, the plan had been simple. According to Benny, the house had been deserted for years, ever since a prison guard had supposedly been murdered there a decade ago. The victim's sister, who had also lived in the home, was now in the loony bin. Sixty-Five Stirrup Iron Road had sat vacant ever since. So at the time, it had sounded like a good opportunity.

Zito and Benny made their living selling scrap metal. They'd started back when both men were still employed by Globe Package Service. Every evening, after a grueling nine-hour shift of loading delivery trucks, they'd sit on Benny's back porch, drinking cans of cheap beer and talking. They then tossed the cans into a fifty-five-gallon drum Benny had swiped from the employee parking lot. Eventually, when the drum was full, they took it to the local salvage yard and sold the contents as scrap aluminum, splitting the meager profits fifty-fifty, and promptly spending both shares on more beer, which equaled more cans. Then they discovered the prices the salvage yard and other recycling centers were willing to pay for metals like copper and brass—and when both men were laid off from their positions a month later with no hope of being called back, they began scrounging metals and flipping them for cash. Brass and copper brought them an especially good payday, but they were also hard to find—legally.

Which was how Zito had gone from blue-collar ne'er-do-well to petty criminal in his thirty-eighth year of life.

They'd started by stealing chopped copper and aluminum plates from the local foundry, but after three such late-night raids, the police had opened an investigation, and the foundry's security guards were extra-vigilant. So then the two men had moved on to stripping abandoned houses, deserted industrial centers, and new homes under construction of their brass and copper fittings, copper pipes, and copper wire. Thanks to the country's ongoing economic crisis, they had plenty of such locations to choose from.

But after six months, their pickings ran slim, and their thefts had begun to make the local news. Neither man wanted to get caught and go to jail. But they also didn't want to end up like "Fishboy Lenny"—the nickname for a former coworker who had lost his job and then his house and now lived among the homeless on the streets, dirty and sick and mumbling random nonsense at uneasy passersby. Nor did they want to graduate to bigger crimes.

Zito and Benny had a friend named Carl who'd supposedly done a few odd jobs for some guys he insisted were connected to the Marano crime family. One night, Carl flashed a wad of cash, told them he was delivering a load of heroin to a Central Pennsylvanian strip club called The Odessa, and then he disappeared. Nobody had seen or heard from him since— and that had been a year ago. Publicly, the police called it an open case, but Zito had heard through the grapevine that privately, the police didn't feel that Carl would ever be seen again. Fishboy Lenny and Carl were both cautionary tales, and Zito thought about them a lot.

Zito wished he had some other talent, some skill that would allow him to earn a living. Writing or acting or playing an instrument. He could move to New York City, live in one of those artistic communes like The Works. Or maybe just a technical skill, like HVAC repair or automobile maintenance or an IT professional. But he didn't know how to do any of these things. He was a grunt, like his father before him.

So, when Benny suggested they broaden the range of their "recycling efforts" to surrounding counties, and suggested this place on Stirrup Iron Road as a potential location, Zito had agreed to check it out. He'd set out on the reconnaissance mission earlier this morning and had driven to the location, intending to scope out the house, verify that it was indeed deserted, and then report back to Benny. If it seemed safe, they'd raid it after dark and strip the pipe and wire.

But it hadn't been safe. Upon his initial drive-by, Zito had been surprised to find two cars in the driveway, along with a recently mowed yard, freshly trimmed shrubbery, curtains in the windows, and other signs of habitation. He'd been just about to write the whole thing off and suggest to Benny that they find another target when he'd seen a man come out of the house. Briefcase and suitcase in tow, the man got into one of the cars and drove away.

But what Zito's eyes had really been drawn to was the woman in the window. She stood there between the parted curtains, watching the man leave. Zito didn't know if she was the guy's wife or daughter or maybe even the maid. All he knew was that he had to have her.

Zito wasn't a rapist. Indeed, the very act of rape was one that had always sickened him in the past. He'd thought it a vile, repugnant thing to inflict upon another human being, ranking right up there with child molestation and animal cruelty. When coming across depictions of rape while watching a movie or reading a book, Zito had always felt uncomfortable, especially if the scene seemed gratuitous.

Yet here he was, thinking about …

Well, thinking about what, exactly? Busting inside the home and raping this woman? No. No, it wasn't that. It couldn't be that. But he felt drawn to her—a desperate, driving need that eradicated all sensible thought. He had to have sex with this woman. It was a compulsion that could not be denied. His cock ached, and he took one hand off the steering wheel and stroked the bulge in his jeans. Maybe the woman felt the same way, he told himself. Maybe she needed it too. If the guy had been her husband, he was obviously going away on a trip of some kind. The suitcase he'd wheeled behind him indicated that. Zito fantasized that it might be like a porno movie. He'd knock on the door under some flimsy false pretense. The woman would answer, dressed in some skimpy, see-through robe, and through the course of conversation would reveal her loneliness and longing. A few meaningful glances and sexually charged double entendres later, they'd be fucking on the couch.

Except that, in Zito's experience, real life didn't work like that.

What the hell was wrong with him? He hadn't even gotten a good look at the woman—just a vague half-glimpse through the gap in the curtains. Enough to intrigue him, but certainly not an eyeful. But now that he thought about it some more, Zito realized the urge had hit him even before he saw the woman. He'd begun feeling horny—unreasonably aroused—upon seeing the house. And now that he was driving away, the sensation lessened again.

Sighing, he found a service road in a nearby stretch of forest and turned the truck around, intent on heading back home. He'd tell Benny the house wasn't abandoned after all, and they'd have to find another place to steal from. But as he passed the house again, the aroused feeling returned. His erection strained against the fabric of his jeans.

Groaning, Zito slowed down and then coasted to a stop directly in front of the home. He surveyed the exterior and his gaze was drawn upward. Had he just seen a flash of movement from the attic window? Maybe it was the woman, watching him, and wishing he'd come in.

He turned the truck around yet again and returned to the service road. Then he pulled into the forest so the truck wouldn't be seen from the main road. The tires crunched over fallen leaves and branches. It wasn't until he reached for the keys in the ignition that he realized he'd been gripping the steering wheel hard enough for his knuckles to turn white. He turned the truck off, pocketed the keys, and after taking a deep breath, got out of the cab. He quietly closed the door, cautious even though there didn't seem to be anyone around who would hear him.

Zito trembled as he walked back toward the house, nearly overwhelmed by a mix of excitement and fear. Each step brought him closer to the home, and his cock throbbed in time with his footsteps. The sensation both thrilled and disturbed him. Zito was surprised to find himself salivating.

Arrianne decided to take a bath rather than a shower. One of the things she'd most been looking forward to since moving into their new home was the luxurious spa-styled bathtub in the master bathroom, with its ornate fittings and plenty of room to stretch out and relax, but between unpacking and the problems with the chipmunks and all the other distractions that had risen from the move, she hadn't yet had a chance to try it out.

Steam rose as the tub filled. Humming, she poured a generous amount of lavender-scented bubble bath and then lit some similarly fragrant votive candles and sat them around the tub's edge and on the sink. Then she lowered the lights until the bathroom was illuminated only by the flickering flames, their reflections dancing in the large mirror over the sink. Arrianne paused, considering whether to turn on some music but then decided against it. Her phone, on which she kept her downloaded music, was downstairs in the kitchen, and she didn't feel like retrieving it. The water simply looked too inviting. She turned the faucets off and tested the water's temperature. It was perfect. Sighing, she eased herself into the tub and leaned back until only her head was above the water. Then she closed her eyes and smiled.

Her thoughts drifted, focusing at first on Chuck and then on all the things she had to do, like calling the IT specialist. And there was still the problem of the chipmunks to deal with, and whatever it was that had been skittering around in the attic. Then her thoughts turned briefly to Teddy, but she forced herself to think of something else, determined not to let that grim memory lead to sadness and ruin this bath—something she'd been looking forward to. Teddy was gone. She'd grieved, but now she told herself it was time to put that grief aside and move on with life. As Chuck had said before leaving, maybe it was time to get a dog.

She tried again to relax, replaying her and Chuck's

previous sexual encounter in her mind. Slowly her fingers found her sex beneath the water. She was tender from her earlier explorations on the couch, but soon the soreness was forgotten, overridden by waves of bliss. When she'd finished, Arrianne had forgotten all about Teddy, and the chipmunks, and the strange porn on her husband's computer. Exhausted, completely relaxed, and relishing the womb-like feel of the water enveloping her, she watched the candles flicker until she drifted off to sleep.

Zito glanced around nervously as he hurried up the driveway. His emotions were still hopelessly conflicted—lust and fear, desire for the woman, and disgust with himself. Deep down inside he desperately hoped a car would come along. If he was spotted, then he would have no choice but to call the whole thing off and return to the truck. But the road remained empty, and there were no other houses close enough that a nosy neighbor would see him. He was alone out here.

And so was the woman inside the house.

No witnesses.

Zito didn't find any piles of dog shit in the yard. Nor were there signs of digging or patches of yellowed grass that would indicate a dog had been pissing there. Zito took a deep breath. His feet felt like bags of wet cement. As he plodded up the steps, his heart throbbed furiously. There were no obvious signs of an alarm system or security cameras. With one trembling hand, he reached out and tried the doorknob. It turned easily. Unlocked.

Okay, he thought. *Now what? You're not a rapist. I mean, you've done some bad things in life, especially lately, but rape? No ... not rape. But I could just peek inside real quick. If I get caught, I can make up a story—rush out of there. And maybe ... maybe she won't* want *me to leave.*

He knew his thought process was irrational—especially the last part, but the compulsion was too strong. He couldn't *not* turn the door handle, and as he did, his stomach acid churned with a sickening mix of excitement and fear. Then he edged the door open and listened. The house was silent.

He opened the door further, looked inside, and saw an empty foyer leading into a living room.

Holding his breath, Zito stepped into the foyer and carefully closed the door until it clicked. Then he stood still, listening and waiting. The house remained still. No barking dog, no voices, no music or television or anything else. An urge came over him to call out a greeting and was quickly followed by an even stronger urge to laugh, but he suppressed both, as well as the compulsion to turn around and leave before he got himself any deeper.

Instead, he moved farther into the home, compelled by some base desire that he did not understand and could not control.

He cautiously explored the first floor and found it deserted. Pulse hammering, Zito licked his lips and crept up the stairs to the second floor. When he reached the landing above, he heard a thumping sound over his head. He froze, senses hyperaware, and the sound came again.

The third floor, he thought. *She's on the third floor.*

Without pausing to explore the second floor, he tiptoed past the open doors of several bedrooms and a closed door that he assumed must lead to a master bathroom, until he reached the end of the hall. The sounds from above grew more insistent. Zito glanced upward and found a string dangling from a trapdoor in the ceiling. He realized that what he'd assumed was a third floor was actually an attic.

Grinning, he reached for the string. He didn't pause to consider how the woman could be up in the attic if the trapdoor was closed. His desire overrode all caution and logic. His loins ached. His body felt tense and electric. He pulled the string and the trapdoor sprang open, releasing a hinged wooden stepladder. Someone had obviously recently oiled the hardware, as neither the door nor the stairs made any sound. The thumping and rustling sounds were louder now, beckoning him upward. Without hesitation, Zito climbed into the attic.

It was dark, but after a moment's fumbling he found a light switch and flicked it on. He spotted haphazard stacks of empty moving boxes and plastic tubs and containers, and a pile of pink fiberglass insulation, but that was all. If the woman he'd seen in the window was up here, she was hiding. He stepped forward, no longer bothering to be quiet.

Then he cleared his throat. "Hello?" he half-whispered. "Don't be scared. I—"

Three things happened at once.

Something slammed into Zito from behind, crushing him face first onto the hard wooden floor. His lips mashed against his teeth and he tasted blood.

The trapdoor whispered shut behind him.

And the light went out, pitching the attic into darkness again, save for a small sliver of illumination bleeding up through a crack in the floor.

Zito tried to shout, tried to move, but found that he couldn't. His muscles seemed frozen. Gripped by some invisible force, he struggled futilely to get away. He felt a presence hovering over him, but he couldn't turn his head to see who it was. He concentrated all his will but couldn't even grit his teeth. All he could manage was a brief twitch of his fingers. More blood filled his mouth. Zito wanted to retch, but he couldn't even do that.

A terrible smell engulfed the attic. Despite the strange paralysis, his stomach muscles convulsed and his breath hitched at the stench. When they were kids, Zito and his buddies used to find dead animals along the side of the road and stuff firecrackers inside the rotting corpses. Then they'd light the fuse, cackling with glee and revulsion as the already splattered road kill got even messier. This smell reminded him of that.

The presence loomed over him, and the air itself felt heavier. Then something plunked down onto the floor next to his head. Zito managed to flick his eyes to the left and glimpsed a box. In the dim sliver of light, he could only read a portion of the carton's lettering—Boroscopic Conduit Inspection System. Then he noticed that one end of the box was open, the flaps clearly bent back. Whatever a Boroscopic Conduit Inspection System was, it had already been removed from the carton.

Zito tried to scream as two powerful hands seized his hips and yanked him to his knees, but he couldn't. Nor could he wipe away his tears as something shredded his jeans and underwear from behind. He felt cool air on his buttocks, and then something slimy and bumpy slid across his exposed flesh. Zito wanted to shudder, but his paralysis prevented even that. The slimy sensation vanished but was replaced seconds later as something cold and hard was pressed against his puckered anus.

Then, there in the darkness, he found out exactly what a Boroscopic Conduit Inspection System was. And while his body couldn't move, it could feel. Indeed, the paralysis seemed to amplify his sensations.

Zito prayed for the paralysis to break, prayed for the ability to scream, and then, finally, he simply prayed for death.

He slipped into shock and then unconsciousness before any of his prayers were answered.

When Arrianne woke, the bathwater was cold and the bubbles had dissipated. Shivering, she glanced around. The bathroom was dark. The candles had burned themselves down to sputtering waxy stubs.

"Jesus," she murmured. "How long was I asleep?"

Her fingertips had wrinkled and her joints were stiff. It took her a moment to climb out of the tub. Doing so sent jolts of pain through her muscles. She sat on the edge, curling her cramped toes onto the fluffy green bathmat, and clenched her teeth until the pain subsided. Then she grabbed a towel and wrapped it around her shivering body. After wrapping her hair in a second towel, she turned the light on and snuffed the remains of the candles out.

So much for relaxing in a bubble bath, she thought. Instead of soothing her, she was now uncomfortable and cold. Shrugging, she bent over and opened the drain. The water rushed noisily down the hole.

Arrianne hurried into the bedroom, finished drying off, and then got dressed. As she slid into her panties, she grew aroused again. Determined not to let herself be distracted, she shoved the urgency aside and headed out into the hall, intent on tackling her to-do list.

In the kitchen, she noticed the Boroscopic Conduit Inspection System box lying on the counter where Chuck had left it the day before. She made a note to remind him to put it away when he got home. Then she began searching for the phone number for her IT team and forgot all about the unit.

A single, muffled thump echoed down from the attic. Arrianne stood still, phone in hand, listening, but the sound wasn't repeated.

"Focus," she muttered. "It's going to be a beautiful day."

Upstairs in the attic, something chuckled softly while Zito's blood congealed on the floorboards and pink insulation.

CHAPTER FIVE
BRIAN KEENE
AND NATE SOUTHARD

After placing a call to her IT team and reporting the recent troubles, Arrianne decided to check her Facebook page. She was lonely—and a little apprehensive. This was her first time alone in the house since they'd moved here, and it felt big and empty and too silent without Chuck. Arousal still hovered in the air around her and only amplified her loneliness.

She opened the app on her phone and posted a status update about falling asleep in the bathtub and how silly she'd felt about it. A few people "liked" the update. A few more commented. She responded to them. Then she checked her husband's Facebook page. Chuck was a social networking fanatic and regularly posted status updates on both Facebook and Twitter throughout the day. Neither had been updated, which meant he was still traveling.

Bored, Arrianne scrolled through her news feed, perusing through the updates of friends and family members—mostly complaints about employers or reports on what people were having for lunch or funny pictures of cats, along with a few birthday and anniversary announcements. This only added to her boredom. It seemed like everybody was having a good time except for her. She checked her YouTube app, but nothing caught her interest there. Then she clicked her news app, hoping to find a distraction. Instead, she found Democrats and Republicans arguing with each other about things she didn't understand—budgets and sequesters and constitutional amendments. Arrianne often wished she could take a larger interest in current events, but every time she tried, she soon found herself overwhelmed with minutia and trivialities. She returned to the Facebook app, but nobody else had commented on her status update.

Restless, Arrianne's thoughts turned to Chuck's suggestion

of adopting a dog. She decided to go online and check the websites of some of the local no-kill pet adoption centers. She closed her Facebook app and opened the phone's web browser. Normally the browser opened to a blank screen, but when Arrianne clicked on it now, what she saw made her gasp.

Three women with stringy, greasy hair knelt around a metal dog bowl. They wore nothing but faded, threadbare panties, and she noticed bruises and burns all over their sallow skin. Black circles shadowed their emotionless eyes. Their ribs pressed hard against their flesh. Each bone was clearly visible. One of them, maybe a blonde after a good shower and a round of antibiotics, sported a busted lip, blood dried to a tacky mess at the corner of her mouth. Another had a black eye. Somebody had abused these women.

As Arrianne watched with wide eyes she desperately wanted to shut, the trio of women reached into the dog bowl and scooped up handfuls of a clear, stringy liquid. She couldn't tell what the substance was, only that it stretched between their hands in thick, sloppy ropes. The women held their hands to each other's mouth, shoved fingers past lips and teeth. She still couldn't tell what the liquid might be.

Then she saw it. At the edge of the screen, a long, thick string of what looked like dog saliva fell from off camera into the dog bowl. Another followed. Her stomach clenched. This was disgusting! What kind of sociopath could possibly get off on something like this?

The women started slathering the handfuls of saliva all over each other's faces and breasts. Cheap mascara smeared. One of the girls slapped the blonde across the mouth. She moaned as though she'd never experienced such pleasure. Arrianne watched as the woman leaned back, her eyes lidded with sensation, and started jamming her fingers into her sex. Her movements were fast and almost brutal, as though she were punishing herself instead of masturbating. She started with two fingers and then went to three. By the time she slid a fourth into herself, Arrianne felt hot tears fill her eyes. The phone shook in her trembling hand.

"Jesus Christ …"

The blonde had her entire hand up herself now. Her wrist jackhammered in and out, and her moans of pleasure became screams of ecstasy. The camera zoomed close. The skin of her wrist was slick with secretions and blood. Then the camera pulled out some, and Arrianne remembered the other two women. One lay on her back. She held a high-heeled shoe in her hands, and the heel disappeared inside her again and again. The other woman kneeled and choked her, knuckles white around her throat.

Drugs, Arrianne thought. *These women are obviously junkies, and this is what they have to do to get cash for their jollies.* She wanted to be sad, but revulsion was the only emotion she could muster.

The video paused as the connection slowed. Arrianne considered closing the app, but before she could, it started again.

The woman doing the choking began to hitch. Her entire body quaked, and a gagging choke clucked out of her throat as her mouth dropped open. Arrianne knew the sound and what it meant, and she frantically punched her phone's power button, trying to shut everything down before she could see the act. Nothing happened. Her phone ignored her, and a thin squeal rushed past her lips as the woman on the screen bent forward and vomited onto her writhing partner.

Panicking, Arrianne rushed to the couch and shoved her phone under the cushions. Though muffled, she could still hear the wet, gagging sounds coming from the device. She stared in horror, wishing she was deaf. What was happening? Could it be some sort of computer virus, infecting not only their home computers but now her phone as well? She thought about calling the IT professionals back, but the noises coming from beneath the couch cushions changed her mind. She didn't want to be anywhere near her phone.

She couldn't handle it anymore. Rushing through the house, she gathered her purse and keys and left the phone where it lay. In the next moment she dashed out the door and into her car. The engine thrummed to life, and she peeled away from the house as quickly as she could, not even caring that she had no destination in mind.

CHAPTER SIX
NATE SOUTHARD

Arrianne drove without direction, the radio turned to a loud rock station. She didn't care for the music much, but it drove out some of the sounds that throbbed in her memory like a horrible taunt.

Breathing deep, she tried to make herself stop shaking. When it was on the computer, she'd been able to tell herself it might have been a virus of some kind, or that maybe somebody had hacked into their Wi-Fi. Even though both were an invasion of privacy, at least they were issues she'd heard of and knew could be corrected. If someone had managed to hack her phone, however, she didn't know what could be done. Would she have to change numbers? Would that even help? How had someone even hacked into her phone, and why would this sick person want to torture her with such disgusting trash?

When she realized her knuckles hurt from gripping the steering wheel too hard, she decided she had to stop somewhere. She looked around and didn't recognize the neighborhood. Then again, what part of the new neighborhood did she recognize? She hadn't paid attention to the various turns she'd made, but she was on a busy street. With any luck at all, she'd find her way home without too much trouble.

On the left was a strip mall. At one end was a sign that said Cedar Door Pub. A relieved breath drifted out of her. Surely she'd earned a drink. Without another thought, she flipped on her blinker and turned into the lot.

She'd seen all sorts of bars over the years, visiting them for everything from work happy hours to birthdays or bachelorette parties. This one was nothing special. Old wooden bar stools with flecks of rust on the legs, light that was somehow both too dim and too bright. The entire place smelled like it had been wiped down with an old rag. She saw a few people in a booth in the back corner, a single man in a mechanic's shirt at the bar. The bartender looked bored, clicking through the channels on a small TV wedged into the corner.

Arrianne sat, and the bartender made his way over at once, plopping down a small paper coaster.

"Happy weekday. What can I get you?"

Would a beer do it? No, she didn't think it would. "Whiskey sour."

"Lady after my own heart."

"You like whiskey sours?"

"Well, I like whiskey. Have that for you in a second." He gave her a half-smile, and she returned it. Already some of the panic-stress had eased out of her. She could take her phone to the cell shop, have it checked out. If it needed a chip replaced or anything, she paid six dollars a month for cell insurance. A couple of steps, and everything would be taken care of. Annoying, sure, but not insurmountable. They could get on with their lives, look at some dogs. Once they found a dog who needed a home and brought him into the house, they'd feel more stable. A family.

Somebody slid onto the stool beside her as the bartender approached, whiskey sour in hand. A little shocked, she turned to see the man in the mechanic's shirt. He held out a ten as the bartender placed her drink on the paper coaster.

"Let me take care of this one," the stranger said.

"That's okay," she said.

"No, let me. You're drinking something strong at this hour, you probably need it. Shouldn't have to worry about paying for it too."

She gave the man a flat look. "Seriously, it's—"

"Please? I try to do a good turn daily. Old Scout motto I can't seem to shake." The mechanic gave her a friendly grin. He was handsome, a little young. Blue eyes sparkled. Grime darkened his fingers, the kind of stains left behind by manual labor. Arrianne smelled oil and rubber, confirming that the man worked on cars in some way.

"Fine," she said. "Thank you." She tilted her glass to him

and then took a sip. Cold liquor sluiced down her throat and immediately warmed her.

"I'm Jake," he said. The patch on his left breast backed him up. He stuck out a hand for shaking and then snatched it back. "Sorry. Not the cleanest right now."

"It's all right. It's a pleasure to meet you, Jake. Arrianne."

"Wow. That's a hundred-dollar name if I ever heard one."

"Don't worry. I got it on sale. It only cost me seventy."

Jake chuckled. "The lady knows a bargain. That's good."

"Never pay full price for something you want," she said. Then she knocked back another swallow. Her cheeks felt a little warm, and she felt the smile on her face like it had never been there before.

"Do you always get what you want?" Jake asked.

She smiled a little wider, gave him a little wink. "As soon as I decide I want it." The words bounced around her mind a moment, and she suddenly felt embarrassed. Jesus, was she flirting with this guy? He'd bought her a drink, and now she was winking at him and talking coy? *Way to live up to that particular cliché,* she thought, and the smile disappeared from her face.

Jake leaned in closer now.

She gave him a tiny shake of her head. "I'm sorry. Thanks a ton for the drink, but I'm not ... I'm in a relationship, so I'm not really up for grabs. Again, I'm sorry. I can pay you back for the drink, it's no problem. Here, let me ..." She reached into her purse and rummaged around for her billfold.

Only a second passed before his hand appeared on her wrist. His grip was gentle, but it was still a grip. So much for not touching her with dirty hands. "I understand. Don't worry about it." He let go and turned to face forward. As he sipped at his beer, he shook his head and chuckled again.

"I really am sorry," Arrianne said.

"Don't be. It's completely fine."

Again, she sipped her drink. The whiskey sour was tasty, and it had already warmed her belly, but her nerves continued to jangle. For whatever reason, Jake wasn't leaving. He continued to sit beside her and sip his beer, even ordering another when the first ran dry. She contemplated getting up and moving, but she didn't want to show the man that he made her nervous. Instead, she finished her drink and ordered another. When Jake didn't offer to pay, she felt more than a little relieved.

The bartender left them alone, and Jake leaned in just a little. He continued to face forward. "Look," he said, "I'm not trying to be an asshole or anything. I'm sorry if I came off that way."

"You didn't."

"Good. It's just … well, obviously you're beautiful. I just thought maybe it was worth a shot. You never know, right?"

"It's okay. And thanks."

"Don't mention it."

Another moment passed. On the TV, Drew Carey was telling somebody how to play Plinko.

Jake leaned in again. Closer, this time. "Okay, so I'm just going to say something. You're fucking beautiful, okay? And fucking hot. I needed to tell you that."

Arrianne fought the urge to shake her head. She had to give him credit for audacity and persistence. "Uh, thanks? This is—"

"I have $50 in my wallet," he said. "It's yours if you want it."

"What?" Was this guy for real? Was he really propositioning her?

"Just … just come out to my car with me for a minute, and it's yours."

She gasped, and then she spoke to him in a harsh whisper. "Are you fucking crazy? You think—what? You think I'm going to come suck your dick or something?"

"No! No, I'm not like that."

"Then what, asshole?"

Jake frantically waved his hands. "Never mind. Just forget about it."

"Oh, fuck that. You put the offer on the table. Tell me what you think I'm going to do to you for fifty goddamn dollars." Rage burned in her chest. She wanted to hit him, just slam her fist into his cheek and hope it did some real damage.

"You wouldn't have to do anything. I just …"

"Just what?"

He blushed a little, and she almost slapped him for it. "It's nothing," he said. "I was hoping maybe … I guess … I wanted you to watch me touch myself."

Arrianne grabbed hold of the bar's edge before she could fall off her stool or throw a punch. This asshole could not be serious. Who did that? Who had the balls to ask a random stranger to watch them jerk off?

As she stared, frozen by shock, Jake reached into his back pocket and retrieved his wallet. He plucked a fifty dollar bill from the leather and held it between two fingers, offering it to her.

Her hands moved before she could stop them. A loud crack split the air as her right hand struck Jake's cheek, and her left hand snatched the bill from his fingers before he could react.

"What the hell?" he asked.

"Consider it asshole tax," she said.

She clutched her purse tight and turned away, stomping toward the door. Not once did she look back. With anger boiling inside her, she climbed behind the wheel of her car and fled the Cedar Door Pub. She wouldn't clear her head there.

She drove aimlessly for more than an hour. Her anger refused to abate. As she steered back to the house, she wanted to hit something. Several times she pounded the heel of her hand against the steering wheel. What the hell was happening with the world? People were throwing up on each other online and asking strangers to watch them jack off. If anybody had told her when she was a teenager that such things were possible, she would've refused to grow up. Something had turned the world sick.

She refused to believe she was a prude. Far from it. She remembered an incident from the first year of her relationship with Chuck. They'd been in a traffic jam, bored out of their wits, and she'd decided to surprise him. He'd thought she was joking even as she pulled his cock from his pants and began to stroke.

When Chuck noticed the semi truck alongside them, he'd moved to stop her, but she swatted his hands away. "Let him watch," she'd said. "Let him be jealous."

The woman who'd jerked off her husband to a trucker's delight couldn't be considered uptight about sex, but she refused to believe that meant any Tom, Dick, Harry, or Jake could just start asking strangers to watch them. And it sure as hell didn't mean she should accept vomiting junkies as sexual entertainment.

She pulled into the driveway and killed the engine. Taking a few deep breaths, she hoped the battery on her phone was dead, that some horrible video wasn't playing on it when she opened the door.

When she entered the house and locked the door, she breathed a small sigh. Silence filled the air, and it sounded perfect. She'd have to get her phone charged before she could have it looked at, and she'd need it to talk to Chuck later, but right now its silence was the best thing she'd ever heard.

Three steps from the door, something came over her. A sudden lust surged through her like a warm tide. She drew in a deep breath, and every inch of her skin tingled. Her anger melted away, and she staggered to the wall, leaning her head against her forearm as she trembled against her sudden need.

It didn't make sense. A portion of her mind told her that even as she unbuttoned her jeans and shoved her fingers inside. There was no time to run a bath or even make her way to the couch. She needed to cum immediately. Her middle and ring fingers slipped inside her already soaked sex, and her entire body shuddered. A gasp escaped her, followed by a moan that was close to a scream.

Frantically, she worked herself with the two fingers. Nothing seemed to be fast enough or hard enough. Everything tingled. Everything burned. The feel of her erect nipples against the fabric of her bra was electric, and she reached under her shirt with her free hand, finding a nipple and pinching. She ground her teeth and whined. Cramps ached in her wrist and forearm, but she ignored them. Something deep inside her began to rumble, building with pressure. Her whine arced upward. She worked her fingers in and out as fast as she could. Her breath caught in her throat.

She hung on the precipice but couldn't fall the rest of the way. Spinning, she pressed her back against the wall. Digging a third finger into herself, she slipped her other hand from her shirt and clamped it around her throat, squeezing hard. Every sensation multiplied. A shocked grin filled her sweat-soaked face. Never had she imagined something could feel so amazing. Stars sizzled at the darkened edges of her vision, and she imagined Jake's hands on her, the bartender watching without interest as he choked her and she pleasured herself.

The orgasm hit her body like a bomb. Arrianne screamed, throwing her head back as her knees buckled and she spilled to the hallway floor. Everything convulsed as the orgasm ripped through her again and again. With each violent rush of pleasure, her legs kicked out. She released her grip on her throat, and her orgasm became more powerful. Without thinking, she slapped herself across the face.

"Fuck!" she screamed as her breath returned. "Mother-fucker!" She'd never felt such a release, never felt anything so powerful. It felt as though every piece of her had rushed away, leaving her body an empty shell. She whimpered as she curled into a ball in the hallway, slipping her fingers free of her jeans. Her hand ached, seized by a cramp she couldn't fight.

"Holy shit," she said into the floor. The first tears came after that. A melancholy unlike any sadness she'd ever felt rushed in to fill the void. She sobbed once, and the questions followed. What was happening to her? To everything? Strange websites. Anger becoming lust in the blink of an eye. How was it possible?

A rotten scent drifted down the hallway. She smelled it and coughed against the back of her hand, her stomach clenching hard. And that was another goddamn thing. Why couldn't they find that stink's source?

"Damn it," she said as she climbed back to her feet and buttoned her jeans. The sadness had departed some, but the anger remained. All she'd wanted to do was look at dogs. How had the day spiraled so completely out of control? Grumbling, she left the hallway and the smell behind. She'd deal with them later.

CHAPTER SEVEN
JACK KETCHUM

Jake didn't know exactly why he followed her. It wasn't the fifty. It wasn't to get the fifty back. It wasn't to apologize. He honestly didn't know. Just as he didn't know why the hell he'd said what he said and did what he did back at the bar.

It wasn't like him. Not at all.

Forget that his mama had raised him to be polite to the ladies.

He'd never asked a woman to do anything *remotely* like that in his life.

Get off on somebody watching?

Never.

He wasn't real adventurous sexually speaking. Jake was straight-on missionary-style. So straight it almost embarrassed him sometimes.

But back at the bar it was as though some other guy had suddenly gained access to his brain. He shared a stiff dick with that guy because this woman Arrianne gave off sex like a fucking lethal toxin, but that was about all he shared.

He'd pay her to watch? Hell, he'd *never* paid for sex. And he could jerk off perfectly well all by himself, thank you very much.

He couldn't believe what he'd said and done.

That was this other guy. Not him.

Yet here he was following her in his pickup for almost an hour now and he didn't for the life of him know why.

It was as though he was meant to do this. As though it were important.

But he also hadn't the slightest idea where the hell she was going, either.

She'd turned off Route 10 onto Cedar Street and driven there for a while past rows of suburban houses clustered on either side, many of them sporting FOR SALE signs on their lawns because out here as almost everywhere the economy still sucked. They then turned on to Royal Avenue and got back on 10 driving south this time, not north like before and then at the next exit got off again. And now she was deep into suburbia once more, and then suburbia running toward rural, driving streets Jake had known since childhood, turning left, right—every which way—and at first he thought maybe she was aware of him behind her and was trying to lose him.

Then, with all the fitful starts and stops, he figured she was just lost. Period.

He lit a cigarette and followed.

Finally, Route 10 north again. And when she exited this time her driving seemed calmer, less erratic. Like she knew where she was now.

He checked his watch. It was quarter after two. Seymour over at the garage would be wanting to skin him right about now for taking this long for lunch. Let him. As a mechanic … Seymour was a very fine typist. Without Jake the place would go to hell in a matter of months.

She slowed and turned onto Stirrup Iron Road. He knew it well.

He paused at the corner.

When she was a few blocks down he turned and crept along behind her.

He had a funny feeling about this. Like something was about to occur.

Something *not good.*

She pulled into a long steep driveway on her left. She was home.

And that was when it hit him full force.

No, not good at all.

He was nineteen when it happened. He'd just landed his first position that wasn't just some pump-jockey over at Teddy Panik's garage, closed now these seven years. He remembered coming home tired and satisfied and happy from work one day and hearing his older brother, Lee's, voice coming from the kitchen.

There was something about the tone.

Lee was sitting at the kitchen table. He was still in his patrolman's uniform but for the hat, which he held in his lap. His mother would never allow hats at the table. His mother's arm rested on his brother's slumped shoulder and she glanced up at Jake's approach and shook her head as though to say *don't speak.*

Lee noticed this and turned toward his brother.

His eyes were brimming over, his face streaked with tears.

Jake had never seen a man cry in his life. Certainly not his brother. The linebacker. The skeet-shooter. The cop.

Jake just stood there. And listened.

Lee had just come from Sam Forrestal's place over on Stirrup Iron Road. He'd been one of the first responders and had seen the whole damn thing. The whole filthy mess. The bloody devastation of a man he'd known all throughout high school and cop school, who he'd had beers with and played darts with at The Bar None Grill, whom he'd kidded about Sam opting for working the pen and not the streets.

His sergeant knew all this and told him to get the hell home for the day. So he did.

He'd helped Nicci into the squad car. Nicci raving about puke and cum. Nicci foaming at the mouth like some rabid animal.

And now he was here in the kitchen with his mother. His mother's hand on his shoulder. Crying out his grief and shock into the still, baked-bread-scented air.

They'll find out who did this, his mother had said. *They'll find out who did this terrible thing.* You'll *find out.* You'll *know.*

They never did.

What happened at Sixty-Five Stirrup Iron Road—Arrianne's home now evidently, her car rolling up the driveway—became first the stuff of local news and gossip and briefly a national sensation, and then, for some but not all, gradually faded from memory.

But Jake remembered that day in the kitchen. Remembered

that—at the end of it, the three of them sitting around the table, hands reaching for one another, grasping, holding tight—he'd cried for his brother.

That he'd cried too.

And now, sitting in his truck, tuned-up engine purring like a lazy housecat, he lit another cigarette and waited.

Waited for what?

Once again he didn't know.

CHAPTER EIGHT
JACK KETCHUM
AND SHANE MCKENZIE

Chuck lay naked in his motel bed, the sheet wound around his thighs, and sipped his Deanston Virgin Oak whiskey. The whisky tasted good but the aftertaste was bitter. Or maybe it was just him.

His three-hour drive to the meeting had taken just an hour. That was because there *was no* meeting. Instead there was Flavia, who now lay beside him smoking her omnipresent Newport. Her tanned sleek body sighed.

"I know it's a cliché," she said, "but honestly, it doesn't matter. It happens sometimes."

"I know it's a cliché," he said, "but not to me it doesn't."

She shrugged. "Lay off the single-malt for a while, maybe. Pop a Viagra."

"Fuck the Viagra. With you I've never needed a Viagra and you know it. Goddamn it."

She stubbed out the cigarette, smiled, and rolled over to him and traced his nipple with her black-painted fingernail.

"Awwww … Papa's feeling sorry for himself, is that it?"

In truth he was. Which was rare. He was a successful, hard-working, happily married man. He enjoyed his work. He loved his wife. There was money in the bank. The new house was terrific.

He had it all. And maybe he'd seen too many French movies when he was a college kid but to his mind, having it all included having a mistress who was even more beautiful and sexy than his sexy beautiful wife.

And Flavia was exactly that. Plus she was younger than Chuck by almost ten years. You couldn't discount that either. But he hadn't been cheating on Arrianne these past six months out of some malaise or discontent, which he supposed would have also been very French. No. He'd been cheating because

66

Flavia had been interested in him from the get-go, and he would have been a fool to have passed on that interest. And he wasn't a fool. So he didn't.

But now.

Now his dick didn't work.

What the fuck?

He found himself thinking about Arrianne. About her newfound sex drive. He pictured her bent over, her tight little asshole loosening for the head of his cock. It had been difficult to get it in at first, and when he tried to force it she'd hissed, reached back, and patted him on the thigh.

"Stay still," she'd said. "Let me do it."

The sound of her spitting into her hand had sent shivers of anxiousness across his flesh. She had reached around, slathered his erection in warm, bubbling saliva, and then backed into him ever so slowly. Once the tight, brown flesh of her anus accepted the full, purple head of his cock, the rest slid in easily.

And then it was heaven. Hot, deep heaven.

"Well, what have we got here?"

Flavia's voice startled him back into the here and now. And in the here and now, the comma that was his flaccid penis had become one hell of an exclamation point. He wanted to make some kind of comment about it, get the dirty talk going again. But he just sort of smiled, shrugged. Gave Flavia a look that said, "Well, would you look at that?"

"Papa Bear ready now? Because Mama Bear wants her porridge." Flavia moaned as she bent down, flicked her tongue over the head of his throbbing cock. It was packed with so much blood he thought it would burst like an overfilled water balloon. Even as Flavia opened wide, let his entire length slide down her throat, his thoughts were still on Arrianne.

And he realized then how much he missed her. God, he fucking missed her bad.

I have to imagine my wife to get it up with my mistress? This is fucking bullshit.

Flavia used one hand to massage his balls, even tickled his taint with the nail of her middle finger. The other hand coasted down to her dripping pussy, and just as she started twirling her fingers over her clit, Chuck pulled out of her mouth.

It had been pressed up against the inside of her cheek, and when he pulled out, it made a *Pbaa* sound. He almost wanted to say *bum bum bum bum.*

"What's the problem?" she asked, still working her clit. The other hand went into her hair, fingers combing through the raven-black strands as she closed her eyes, bit her lip, and moaned deep.

When Chuck sat up and reached for his boxer shorts, Flavia's lust-soaked expression melted into a frown. Her glistening fingers pulled away from her groin, and she crossed her arms over her breasts, bared her teeth in a way that gave her a slight under-bite. Not a great look for her.

"Are you fucking serious right now?"

"I'm sorry. I need to get home. This ... I can't do this shit anymore." Zipping his pants over his engorged cock was tricky, and he spied Flavia staring at the bulge that ran along his inner thigh. "You won't be seeing me again. I'm fucking married, for Christ's sake. I don't know what the hell's wrong with me."

Flavia's expression changed again, this time a raised eyebrow and a smirk. "I don't believe this shit. You're going to blow me off for your ugly fucking cunt wife?"

Chuck was about to defend Arrianne, but he didn't see the point. He did his best to ignore Flavia as he gathered his things, though her stare felt like an open oven. "I'm sorry. This was a mistake."

Flavia smiled then. "Don't think so, honey. I'll be seeing you. And if I don't? You'll be seeing me."

Chuck nearly downed another whiskey for the road but slammed the cup on the end table, shattering it. Blood welled in his palm, and he ripped a pillowcase free and wrapped it around his hand. "You stay the fuck away from me and my wife. It doesn't have to be like that, Flavia. I'm sure there're men throwing themselves at you every day, right? Men much younger than me. Go be young. Let me go be old, okay?"

Chuck didn't get a response from her as he finished

dressing. But her stare never left him, and he felt himself start to sweat under its heat. And that fucking smirk never lifted from her lips.

Chuck made his way to the door, back slightly hunched because of the still rock-hard erection in his pants. He shot one last look at Flavia, wanted to say something else, something that would convince her to leave him be. But no words would come.

He turned his back to her and exited the room. Full of guilt. Full of shame. Full of sparkling lust for his wife's embrace.

"See you soon, Papa Bear."

Chuck slammed the door and hurried to his car. The pillowcase was nearly soaked through. Cut must have been deeper than he thought.

He had no idea what he was going to tell Arrianne when he got home. Didn't have an excuse handy as to why he was showing up at home early when he was supposed to be out of town on business.

I'll just tell her the meeting was canceled. No ... I'll tell her I missed her too bad and blew the whole thing off. Fuck ...

At that point he would tell her whatever she wanted to hear to get that ass back in the air. His foot was heavy on the gas pedal as he sped back toward Sixty-Five Stirrup Iron Road.

CHAPTER NINE
SHANE MCKENZIE

Arrianne paced the house. She couldn't figure out what to do with herself. Traces of her explosive orgasm still prickled her skin, and just thinking about it made her want to drop to the floor and kick her pants off. Her thoughts suddenly went back to Jake, and she found herself wondering how long his cock was, what kind of face he would make as he stroked it in front of her.

What the fuck is wrong with me!

She plopped down on the couch, reached for one of the pillows, pressed it to her face, and screamed. The release felt good, but unease still filled her head. She felt something beneath her butt. Reaching beneath the cushion, she retrieved her cell phone. The screen was black. She knew she would have to charge it soon, just in case Chuck tried to call or text her, but she found herself scared to even touch it. Just looking at it conjured images of the dirty, skinny women coating each other in ribbons of gelatinous dog drool, and then her mind became a slideshow of filthy flesh and streams of vomit and skinny vagrant cock.

Her stomach bubbled, and an acidic burp popped out, burned the back of her throat. She scanned her surroundings and suddenly felt very alone, very vulnerable. And dirty. She felt so goddamn dirty that she just wanted to wrap her fingers around her throat again, wanted to rub her clit while she watched Jake jerk himself off.

If he were here now, I'd do a lot more than watch.

Her feet carried her toward the front door, and though she couldn't believe she was having these thoughts—especially after the titanic nut she just busted—it didn't stop her from massaging her sore, chaffed groin as she parted the curtain and peered out into the yard.

A pickup truck sat down the road, just close enough that she could make out a male driver. His arm hung out the window and his face was aimed at her front door. Spirals of cigarette smoke drifted from his nostrils, and a smile spread across his face.

Jake?

She gasped, yanked her hand away from herself, and backed away from the window. *No,* she thought. *He isn't really sitting there. It's my own fucked-up imagination. It's this goddamn house messing with my head.*

She gave herself a couple of minutes to collect herself, took a deep breath, and then spread the curtain just wide enough for her eye.

The truck was gone.

She wanted to feel relief, but instead waves of disappointment crashed over her. She wanted him to be out there, wanted him to come inside and fuck her.

What? No ... no I don't.

Her hands were balled into hard fists, and she clenched her teeth as she growled in frustration. She leaned against the door and stared at the ceiling, wanting nothing more than for Chuck to come home, hold her in his strong arms, tell her she wasn't crazy.

A walk. That's what I need. Some fresh air.

She swung the door open and slammed it, crossed her arms, and chewed her tongue as she briskly walked away from the house and toward the lake. Just across from the road was a beaten trail, and she followed it into the trees, feeling better already.

Jake crept the truck through the heavily wooded area close to the house, looking for a good place to park it so it was out of sight.

When the woman's face had suddenly appeared in her window only minutes before, he knew he should have been concerned, at the very least embarrassed. But all he could do was smile at her. She was just so goddamn pretty. His cock nudged at the underside of his zipper as he pictured the woman

71

on her back, naked, fingers knuckle-deep in pussy meat. And he knew he had to have her. Nothing could stop him from tasting her.

The second her face had disappeared from the window, he had backed the truck up and took off down the road. Almost every part of his brain had told him to get the hell out of there, get as far away from this woman's house as possible, go back to work like he was supposed to.

Almost every part of his brain told him this. But he didn't. Because the part of his brain that disagreed with the rest was stronger, and it told him to stay close, wait for the bitch to leave. It told him that once she was gone, he could break into the house, hide out, wait for her to get back. He hadn't seen her leave the house, but that part of his brain knew somehow. And when she got back, he could fuck her. He could fuck her so long and hard that she would never want him to stop.

Fuck her? But I can't do that ... I can't even jack off in front of her ...

But that part of his brain told him he could. He could fuck her in every hole, could fuck her until she bled. It didn't take long before that part of his brain had convinced him it was right, and he grinned until his cheeks ached.

I can *fuck her. She* wants *me to fuck her.*

He came across another truck, parked amongst the trees. He wondered if this Arrianne had other admirers, which wouldn't surprise him in the least. This girl was fine. Damn fine.

A husband maybe? Boyfriend?

It wouldn't matter either way. She was going to be his, no matter who was in the house. If he had to take care of some asshole to get what was his, he would take care of said asshole, no problem.

After he parked his truck beside the other, he hopped out, stuck his head in through the other's window, but found it empty for the most part. There were some tools, some empty food wrappers and soda bottles.

The truck didn't matter. Only Arrianne mattered. Another cigarette found its way to his lips, and he lit it as he trudged back toward the house on foot.

***

Arrianne couldn't help but smile as she strolled along the trail. The surrounding trees swayed in the breeze and gave off a piney scent that filled her with calm. Birds sang songs for her and butterflies danced through the air. Her mind cleared and she felt more relaxed than she had in a very long time, and the tranquil feeling only seemed to increase with every step she took away from the house.

And for the first time today, she felt like she had her thoughts together. Her *own* thoughts. She wasn't thinking about fingering or choking herself, wasn't thinking about Jake's penis or vomit or high heels or dog saliva baths. She felt like herself, and she took a long, deep breath as she continued her trek through the woods.

She figured it had to just be stress that was causing her to act out, that was putting all that garbage into her head.

Things will get better, she told herself. *Don't go losing your shit, Arrianne.*

She stopped for a moment, leaned up against a tree. A squirrel chattered at her from a limb just above her head, pouncing from left to right as if challenging her.

"What's your problem?" she said, and then chuckled as the squirrel grew more agitated, squeakily cussing her out in its squirrel language. She wondered if this was a mother squirrel protecting her young, and the mother rat from their old home burst into her mind, yellow teeth bared and blood-stained. A shudder tickled her flesh, and she only stared at the hysterical rodent for another few seconds before moving on down the trail. As the images of the crazed rat began to fade, her mind drifted to the scratching sounds coming from the attic, the chipmunks that were building a well-hidden nest in there somewhere. She only hoped they could find them and get rid of them without having to hurt the poor things.

Thinking about the rat naturally brought Teddy to mind. The way his eye had been hanging from his socket, his fur all matted with blood. Teddy used to love to climb trees, and she knew if he was there now, in their new home surrounded by

73

pines, they would have all sorts of shredded, furry gifts at their doorstep on a daily basis. A tear fattened at the corner of her eye, and she wiped it away, forced a laugh.

She was almost at the lake now, saw it sparkling through the trunks.

Should have brought my swimsuit, damn it.

She thought about going back to the house for it but then decided if the urge to take a dip was strong enough, she'd just strip down and dive in.

Then something rustled the bushes just to her left.

She flinched, put her hand to her chest. "Hello?"

There was a high-pitched sound, and then more rustling.

Arrianne cursed herself for not bringing something to defend herself with. *What if it's a cougar or something?* She searched the forest floor for a weapon, anything she could use. Before she had the chance to bend down and grab anything, the furry body burst from the bush and straight for her.

The scream that trumpeted from her throat was quickly cut off when the dog limped across the trail. A mutt, dark brown with scattered black spots—male. If the dog had an owner, he hadn't bothered getting him neutered. The dog whined as he approached her, his front left paw curled up to his chest.

"What happened to you?" Arrianne asked as she squatted and placed a gentle hand on the dog's head.

His tail got to wagging, and he licked her fingers, stared up at her with soft, pathetic eyes. The dog had no collar, no tags. His eyes had a milky film, and his muzzle was graying. Arrianne could tell this dog was old; she guessed twelve years or so.

She ran her nails along its back, scratched behind his ears. He whined some more, tucked himself between her legs, reached up with his snout, and licked her on the neck.

"Okay, okay," she said as the dog pushed forward and continued flicking its tongue at her. She laughed, scratched under his chin with one hand, and inspected his paw with the other, gently wrapping her fingers around the leg and extending it toward her. "It's okay, boy. You'll be all right."

The dog cried but allowed her to study his leg. There

was no blood, no sign of any injury. *Probably just old age,* Arrianne thought. *Arthritis maybe.*

The dog sat on its haunches, licked her hand, his tail kicking up dust as it wagged.

"You're just an old sweetheart, aren't you?" She stood, crossed her arms. "You want to come home with me? Take a bath, get something to eat? I sure could use the company."

The dog stood, curled that front leg back up, but stared up at Arrianne with what she could only describe as a smile. He panted happily, spun in a circle, and barked.

"I'll take that as a yes," she said, and reached down to pet him on the head again. "Think I'm going to call you Dickey. Does that sound good, boy?"

She took it slow at first, thinking the dog would be slow-going with his gimp leg, but the dog had mastered running with his limp, and he sprinted ahead of her and toward the house.

The door was unlocked and Jake let himself in. He knew Arrianne wasn't there, though he wasn't sure why he knew. The fact was just there in his brain, and there was no doubt it was true.

He shut the door and stood there, taking in the house with his eyes and nose. Sniffing, he picked up on a scent that sent swirls of excitement into his scrotum, up the shaft of his cock. Pussy. No doubt about it. Smelled fresh too.

She knew I was coming, that's what. Getting it ready for me.

Jake took a little stroll around the place, the images of Arrianne's nude body clearing to make room for his brother. Lee had been so upset when he talked about what happened in that house, and now there Jake was, standing in the middle of it, right in the cream filling. He had never met Sam or Nicci, didn't even know they had existed until Lee was crying about them, talking about puke and cum. And lots of blood.

Wonder where all the shit went down.

His feet carried him through the living room and deeper into the house. He stood in front of a den, what appeared to be some kind of computer room, the monitor only a black screen. The air was electrified there. It felt like invisible spiders were scuttling over his skin, and he rubbed at his arms as he glared inside.

There was a series of beeps, followed by a humming sound. The little green light in the lower right corner of the screen lit up, and Jake took a step into the den as the computer continued booting up.

Puke and cum and puke and cum and puke and cum and lots of blood ...

The words popped in his mind like black cats, and his cock responded as he stepped closer and closer to the monitor.

There was no desktop that popped up on screen. It went straight to a website.

PETA: Pets Entering That Ass.

Jake chuckled at the title at the top of the screen, and his smile only grew as the first video played. A woman lay on her stomach, twisting her nipples and screaming through clenched teeth. Though she appeared to be experiencing pleasure, her expression reminded Jake of someone taking a shit. Her face was maroon, veins bulging at her temples and neck.

The camera moved away from her face and circled to the rear, getting a clear shot of her gaping asshole. It pulsated, opened and closed like a wrinkled, whistling mouth.

Jake reached down and squeezed his erection as the woman's anus opened wide, and something dark began to slither out.

She is taking a shit. Why the fuck am I enjoying this?

He didn't know, but he couldn't look away. As the tube slid out farther, a tongue flicked out of the tip, and then he saw the eyes, the scaly skin. That turd was a fucking python, and as it pushed its way out of the woman's bowels, inch by fattening inch, the woman moaned and humped the air. A thick, white mucus coated the snake's skin, and it just kept coming out as if there was no end to its length.

No time for this. She's coming home soon.

He had to hide. He didn't want to ruin the surprise.

He made his way upstairs and didn't have to look far

before he spotted the string hanging from the ceiling. The attic would be perfect. He could wait it out up there, let her get comfortable, and then kick the stairs down and introduce her to *his* pet python. And he knew exactly where he'd put it first.

As quickly as he could he yanked the string, ascended the stairs, and pulled them back up. A childish giggle escaped his lips as he sat in the dark. It would have been pitch black if it wasn't for the LCD screen oozing pink luminescence just a few feet away.

What the fuck is that?

He crawled toward it to inspect.

"Well, come on, boy. Dickey, what's the matter?" Arrianne stood just inside the house, but the dog wouldn't cross the threshold. He sniffed the air and whined, tail tucked between his legs. "Aren't you hungry? I've got some leftover chicken in the fridge. All yours if you come inside."

Dickey licked his chops, gave another long whine, and then finally stepped into the house. His tail stayed tucked as he tentatively walked deeper into the home, eyes ping-ponging in every direction as if expecting something to jump out and attack.

"Believe me, I know the feeling," Arrianne said as she led Dickey into the kitchen. "But we have each other for company now, right?"

Dickey panted and smiled but never lost his defensive stance. He wedged himself between Arrianne's calves as she rummaged through the refrigerator, snatched the Tupperware full of grilled, boneless chicken thighs, and set it on the floor.

"Bon appetite, buddy. Dig in."

Dickey didn't hesitate. He buried his face in the cold meat, gorging himself. His tail finally unsheathed itself and got to wagging again.

"There we go. And when you're done there, I'll run a bath for you. You won't like it, I'm sure, but you'll feel so much better afterward."

Dickey made quick work of the chicken, and she tossed the Tupperware into the sink. She then led him up the stairs toward the master bath. The dog had his head lowered, leg curled up to his chest as he hopped along, eyes darting.

Arrianne ran the water, letting it get nice and warm. She didn't have any dog shampoo, so she would have to use her Pantene on him. As she waited for the tub to fill up, she sat on the edge, ran her fingers through Dickey's fur. With only a single parting of his hair, she saw countless fleas and a few ticks attached to his pink skin.

"Oh, Dickey. These things must be driving you crazy." She pulled him close and scratched his chin, behind his ears. "I think we need to get you to a vet, let them polish you up, don't you?"

Dickey whined, licked her hand.

"Well, let's wash you off first, okay?"

The dog didn't put up a fight as she lifted him into the tub. His eyes stayed on the open door as Arrianne scrubbed him, lathered him up as best as she could. The surface of the water swam with fleas before long, their tiny legs thrashing as they attempted to swim back to their furry home.

Arrianne pulled Dickey out of the water, pulled the plug, and watched the bugs swirl down the drain.

"We'll see what the vet can do about those ticks, okay, buddy? Maybe we can do something about your leg too."

She toweled him off and then led him to the bedroom. Complete exhaustion suddenly took her, and she wanted nothing more than to crawl into bed and pass out. The feeling swept over her out of nowhere, and at that moment, a nap seemed like an absolute emergency.

Her body hit the mattress and bounced, and then she grabbed an extra pillow and tucked it between her thighs. Dickey stood at the edge of the bed by her face and poked his cold, wet snout into her neck.

"I know, buddy. Just ..."—she yawned—"let me rest for a little while, okay? And then after ... after we'll ... go and ..."

Jake stared at the screen, crawled on his knees until he was right in front of it, and held it with both hands. It felt like a gun, and he couldn't for the life of him figure out what was displayed on the screen as he stared at the image. It looked like some kind of pink, fleshy tunnel, wrinkled and venous, with some mud on the walls and floor.

What the fuck is this?

He crawled closer still, and his knees collided with something. His lids fluttered and he backed up a bit as his sight began to adjust.

The light floating out of the screen outlined what appeared to be a body. It lay on its stomach, arms and legs spread out like a starfish. The gun-like device with the LCD on it was pressed up against the man's ass, all the way to the tip. It was then that he realized what he was looking at on the little monitor, and he couldn't help himself from giggling.

So this is what Arrianne does to her admirers, huh? I like that.

A small voice at the back of his head screamed. It was his voice, his real voice. It shrieked, pleaded with Jake, told him this wasn't him, that he would never do anything like this, wouldn't even think like this. It told him something was very wrong, that he needed to get the fuck out of that house now.

But Jake didn't want to hear that. He grabbed hold of the device, pulled on it. It gave some, slid out of the dead man's ass. It just kept coming, reminded him of the mucus-coated python from the video as he pulled it out bit by bit. The smell that came with it induced a fit of gags, but he yanked on the slimy cord until he had all of it out and then wiped his hands on the man's pant leg.

"Now what were you doing with this up your—"

Something heavy landed on his back, squashed the air out of him in an instant. The thick scent of decay was just as heavy, nearly made him puke the second it entered his nasal passages. He tried to move but couldn't, tried to breathe but could only manage enough to catch whiffs of the putrid odor. The voice inside his head screamed again, and he tried to scream with it but couldn't make the sound come out.

The weight on his back pushed harder, so hard he thought his spine would snap and his organs would ooze out of his mouth and asshole like purple toothpaste. Jake wanted nothing more than to look back at who was on top of him but couldn't even will his eyes to turn.

A hand gripped the back of his head like it was no bigger than a baseball, shoved his face into the floor. His nose crunched, gushed blood into a puddle around his face. His front teeth cracked, broke free from his gums, stabbed into his lips as the hand pushed harder. He would have choked on blood if he could have breathed, but all he could do was concentrate on the pain. The heavy, crushing pain. After a few more seconds, his face was lifted off the floor by his hair, blood pouring and splashing below him.

The man's corpse moved then. Jake's eyes were fixed on it, and, since he had no choice, he watched as it was pulled backward toward his face. The scent of shit and death entered his shattered nose and mouth, and the wet, shredded backside of the dead man pressed hard up against his face.

Whatever was on top of him gripped the back of his neck, squeezed like it was trying to pop his head off. It shoved forward, pushed the top of Jake's head against the dead man's ass until he thought his scalp would split.

The grip released him. He saw two dark hands—long and almost fin-like—extend past his head and grip the ass by both cheeks. Next came the ripping sound, like fabric being torn, and something cold and wet slapped Jake in the face, stung the open wounds as it oozed into his broken nose, into the craters on his gums where his teeth once sat.

Then the hand gripped his neck again. Shoved him forward again.

There wasn't as much resistance this time. His head entered the wide-open ass all the way up to his shoulders. What little air he was getting through his nose was quickly cut off, and he wanted to thrash his arms and legs in panic as his lungs starved for oxygen.

Pressure at his rear. Fingers dug in, parted his ass cheeks with a violent rip. Jake wanted nothing more than to scream as his flesh parted and his asshole became a bleeding canyon.

Then there was a snapping sound. Jake could tell from inside the dead man's ass that the body was being moved, bent backward maybe. His own head was pulled back, stretching his neck, nearly popping his head free, but his chin caught and held him in his rectal prison.

More pressure at his rear. Then something entering. Something as big and round as a head. The hair tickled his raw, open flesh, and then teeth scraped across as the head was shoved in.

That part of his brain that had coaxed him into the house was gone now. It was just him now. Just Jake. And all he knew was pain and torture.

"Hck, hck, hck…hhhauck …"

The warm splashes woke Arrianne from a deep sleep. She woke on her back, but the second her eyes popped open and she tilted her chin toward her chest, she was stuck that way. Her body refused to move anymore, was petrified in its current position on the mattress.

Dickey stood on three legs above her, his injured foot curled up and shaking. He whined, ribbons of white and pink drool stretching from his panting mouth. His entire body trembled, the muscles in his legs tight and twitching, the veins bulging like worms twisted around his appendages.

Then his belly heaved, and the noise came again.

"Hck, hck, hck…hck … hhhauck …"

Another wave of warmth splashed down on Arrianne's chest and stomach, ran down her sides and slid into her neck, rode the creases until soaking into the sheets beneath her.

Body parts.

It took Arrianne a moment to gather her thoughts and make sense of what she was watching. Hairy, bloody body parts were rushing out of Dickey's mouth and coating her in bile and sludge. Furry chunks. Splintered bone. Blood and meat.

Arms, legs, paws … heads.

If one of the little creatures wasn't whole, she would have never figured out what kind of animal these parts used to belong to. The creature lay on its side, long black stripes running down its back. It barely had fur, just a thin layer of brown covering the pink skin. It squeaked, wriggled, scraped Arrianne's belly with its tiny claws.

It's a ... it's a baby chipmunk.... Oh, Jesus ...

"Hck, hck ... hhhauck ..."

Another pink, red, and yellow waterfall exploded from Dickey's throat, splashed against her flesh and covered the baby chipmunk in the frothy liquid. It squealed, writhed, crawled its way down Arrianne's naval.

The fresh vomit sizzled as the tiny bubbles popped. Dickey coughed, deep and thick, licked his chops and whined. His body continued to shake. Hair fell off like dead pine needles, floated down to Arrianne's puke-covered torso and stuck there. Tiny fleas scurried across her flesh, swimming in the muck.

The chipmunk kept squeaking, screaming for its mother. Screaming for a warm place to hide.

As it crawled farther down her body, it found that place.

Noooo! Oh God ... nononono!

The baby chipmunk backed into her. She could tell because as it entered her, its frantic squeaking never lost its volume. Its tiny claws bit into her pussy lips as it backed in, having no trouble fitting its tiny body into its new, warm hole.

The mattress moved, springs screeched. Someone had just sat down behind her. Then a hand was in her hair, petting her, scraping its nails across her scalp.

None of this could really be happening, she knew that. This wasn't possible. This kind of thing was only possible in nightmares.

Please wake up ... wake up, wake up, wake up!

A low, deep grumbling chuckle behind her. The petting became heavier, pulling her hair, pressing down on her scalp so hard her eyes watered. The hand was damp, wetting her hair as it stroked her.

She wanted to scream, wanted to run as fast as she could. She wanted Chuck.

The chipmunk burrowed deeper into her, its entire body inside her now. She could still hear the squeaking, but barely. The baby's claws kept digging in, scraping, scratching.

Dickey whined again, long and high-pitched. It looked

like he wanted to get down off the bed but couldn't, as if he was being held there by some invisible force.

And then Arrianne noticed the dark red erection obtruding from between his legs. Threads of matted hair twisted from the end, and the goddamn thing just kept growing.

Dickey hunched his back, repositioned his back paws.

The baby chipmunk burrowed as deep as it could and then began gnawing on the surrounding walls of flesh.

The hand was all nails now, clawing away layers of scalp flesh with every swipe.

Dickey awkwardly began humping. Since Arrianne was on her back, he couldn't get the right angle to enter her, but the hot, red, hair-ridden member jabbed at her stomach, knocked chunks of furry flesh to plop onto the mattress.

Dickey began panting as he humped, pumping and pumping, balancing himself on three legs. He never stopped whining. More drool threaded off his mouth and dripped onto Arrianne's chest.

The dog repositioned himself again, trying to lower his body. He still couldn't get the angle to fuck her, but as he thrust at her stomach, now poking her in the belly button, his furry nut-sack swung and slapped against her cunt.

Slap slap slap slap slap ...

The baby chipmunk responded to the thumping sound by pushing itself deeper, rolling around and clawing. It felt like it had sprouted spines along its body and was spinning in place, shredding her from the inside.

Then Dickey's whines became screams and his tongue hung low from his mouth.

Hot splashes hit her in the belly and chest, some spraying up to her chin and lips. The hand violently caressing her head moved to her mouth, propped her lips and teeth open. Dickey sprayed his seed in hot spurts, globs of it splashing into her mouth, coating her tongue in a salty, biscuit-batter flavor.

When Dickey finished, his legs shook so bad that he fell off the bed backward, landing with a thud.

The stew of fluids and chunks congealed on her flesh, clung to it like hardening Jell-O. She wanted to cry, wanted to curl up and die. Hell couldn't possibly be this bad.

What did I do to deserve this? Why is this happening to me?

The baby chipmunk stirred again, and she felt it crawling its way back out. Every step was pure agony. She knew it poked its head out because there was another series of squeaks.

And then a low growl.

The chipmunk quickly backed its way into her again, screaming and clawing.

Dickey thrust his snout forward, penetrated Arrianne, and chewed his way deeper and deeper, desperate to get to the furry treat inside.

The hand was back on her head, petting. When another chuckle rattled out, Arrianne thought she felt her sanity snap clean in half.

CHAPTER TEN
SHANE MCKENZIE
AND WRATH JAMES WHITE

Chuck pulled into the driveway and shook his head. He ran his hand through his hair and tried to chew down the guilt that had been building strength the entire drive home. The whole Flavia escapade had been such childish bullshit, and now that his mind wasn't muddled with sperm back up, he could see that clearly.

I'm a complete jackass.

Flavia's words wouldn't stop ringing in his head. *I'll be seeing you. And if I don't? You'll be seeing me.*

He knew that crazy bitch would go through with some psycho shit like that. If she showed up at his home, he just might kill her.

"Well, are you ready to check out your new digs?" He looked over at the puppy curled into a ball in the passenger seat. It had been an impulse buy. A Mexican couple in a beat-up old pickup were selling them on the side of the road. The man held a cardboard sign with the misspelled words PUPYS FOR SELL.

The man had told Chuck the dogs were golden retrievers, but he very much doubted they were purebred. Not that it mattered. The little bastard was cute as a button, and Chuck just knew Arrianne would fall in love with it the moment she laid eyes on it.

The puppy whined, hiding its face behind its tiny paws.

"Come here, little guy. Let's introduce you to the missus." Chuck climbed out of his car with the puppy tucked under his arm, his injured hand hanging uselessly, holding his briefcase with the other. He hoped he didn't look too guilty. Every excuse he had come up with on the drive sounded guilty as hell to him.

God, please get me out of this shit. If you do, I'll never look at another piece of ass again.

85

He just stood there, staring at his door. The butterflies in his stomach felt more like a tornado.

Here goes nothing.

The second the door opened, something pounded from the second floor.

"Arrianne!" He dropped his briefcase and sprinted for the stairs, taking them two at a time. The puppy nearly flew from his grasp as he stormed toward the bedroom, but he held on, his heart hammering away at his ribcage.

When he entered the bedroom, he did drop the puppy. It landed awkwardly on its feet, let out a sharp yelp, and then scurried across the floor toward the corner.

Arrianne lay on her back on the bed, completely naked and covered in a glistening layer of sweat. Her head was tilted back, mouth stretched as wide as it would go. Her hands were claws, scraping across her chest and stomach as her feet kicked.

A dog sat by the edge of the bed. It looked old, injured. It held its paw up by its chest and stared at Arrianne with a tilted head. It looked up at Chuck and began panting, smiling up at him.

"Arrianne ... what ... what the hell is going on?"

Arrianne lay on the bed, convulsing, mouth open, gagging. She almost looked like she did when she was ... Chuck pushed the thought from his mind, chiding himself. It was just his penis talking. He'd been thinking about making love to his beautiful wife all day, and now, seeing her naked, sweating, undulating in some bizarre parody of ecstasy, his mind could not separate her obvious distress from the sexual tension that had been building in him for hours.

He rushed to the bed and seized Arrianne by the shoulders. He snatched her up and shook her. "Arrianne! Wake up! Wake up!"

Arrianne's eyes fluttered open. Her pupils swam around in her head, unfocused, before fixing on some point just over Chuck's shoulder. That's when she began to scream. The sound pealed out of her, increasing in intensity until it felt like it would shatter his eardrums. Then it stopped. Her eyes finally found his. She touched him—his face, chest, arms. Then she ran her hands over her own chest and belly, looking around, her expression twisted, eyebrows furrowed, nostrils flared, scowling like she'd just tasted something repulsive and was trying to hold down her bile ... and failing.

Like the scream that had proceeded it, the vomit exploded from her mouth and seemed to go on forever. An endless deluge of half-digested food in yellow and orange chunks coated Chuck's lap faster than he could retreat. He sprang from the bed like it was on fire.

"Jesus Christ! Are you sick or something? What the hell have you been eating?"

She looked stricken. "It ... it wasn't me. The dog! Dickey, he vomited all over me! It ate the chipmunks and threw up all over me! Then he ... he came in my mouth!"

Chuck was already in the bathroom peeling off his vomit-soaked pants and shirt. "He what? Did you just say you sucked off that mutt?"

"No! I couldn't move. I felt like I was paralyzed or something, and Dickey was humping the air right near my face and my mouth was open. He ejaculated in my mouth!"

"You were just dreaming, Arrianne. That dog was cringing in the corner, scared out of his wits. Where the hell did he come from anyway? I thought we agreed on a golden retriever?"

In the other room, still sitting on the bed, Arrianne was breathing hard, eyes open wide, trembling.

"Are you okay? Maybe you *are* sick. Do you have the flu?"

"No! There's something wrong. Something is wrong with this house. That wasn't just a dream. I never have dreams like that!"

Chuck wet a washcloth and washed his chest, legs, and stomach. The foul-smelling yellow effluence had soaked through his underwear. He shook his head and walked over to run the shower, slipping out of his underwear, relieved to have an excuse to wash off Flavia's smell. After spending time with her, he was always paranoid that Arrianne could smell the other woman's sweat and vaginal musk on his skin. Not that it was an issue this time, he realized, since he'd only gotten a blowjob.

"It could be food poisoning," he offered. "People have crazy dreams when they have food poisoning. And you did throw up."

"It wasn't fucking food poisoning!"

"Okay. Okay. Don't get so worked up."

Arrianne got up and stripped the sheets from the bed. Chuck stepped into the shower. He could still hear Arrianne trying to talk to him as she gathered the laundry, telling him how the house made her feel like she wasn't herself, like she was possessed by some nymphomaniac, and how she kept seeing things on the Internet and on her smartphone with the repeated themes of perverse sex and regurgitation and now she was dreaming about it and she was vomiting and there were gerbils or chipmunks or something inside her pussy and the dog had tried to chew them out of her and blah blah.

He leaned his head under the showerhead. The spray drowned out the sound of his wife's hysterical voice. For a long moment, he just stood there, under the showerhead, grateful for a moment of peace, an escape from Arrianne's vomit-phobic ramblings. He wondered if she were losing her fucking mind.

Being stuck with some lunatic was one of Chuck's worst fears. Women were crazy enough by his estimation. All that estrogen fucked up their minds and made them irrational. Trying to speak logically to a woman was like trying to speak Portuguese to a goldfish or a rabid shark. There was just no reasoning with them even on their best days. The idea of his wife losing even that tenuous grasp on reality she normally maintained was terrifying. He liked to think he'd be the loyal and dutiful husband who stayed by her side and made sure she took her medications and spoon-fed her lukewarm porridge and pureed veggies or whatever they feed nut jobs in the nuthouse and wiped the drool from the corner of her mouth and told her love stories and poems and waited patiently for her sanity to return. But Chuck knew himself too well. He wasn't loyal to Arrianne when she was sane. The idea of playing nursemaid to a drooling madwoman terrified him. As much as he wanted to be a good man, a good husband, Chuck knew he was a fucking asshole when it came right down to it. He was good at rationalizing his indiscretions to himself and concealing them from his wife and others, but the fact remained that he was far from husband of the year. He had just left his mistress's bed, for fuck's sake. He bought his wife flowers and jewelry out of guilt. He acquiesced to most of her wishes for the same reasons and let her win most of their arguments, apologizing even when he didn't know what he was apologizing for. He kept the peace at home and let out his frustrations in Flavia's tight little pussy or her toned, perfectly sculpted ass or between her big, perky tits or down her bottomless throat. After a few hours of sexual gymnastics with Flavia, he was agreeable to just about anything. It was all an act and it had everyone fooled, but Chuck couldn't fool himself. If Arrianne went loony, he'd be out of there like the fat kid in dodge ball. He hoped it would never come to that.

Hopefully it was just stress and food poisoning. He'd pick up Ipecac and some Xanax and everything would go back to some semblance of normal. He imagined her getting her stomach pumped at the emergency ward, forced to projectile vomit into a pail, and he thought again about how puke had suddenly become a major theme in their lives. Maybe Arrianne had a point. Things had definitely gotten strange since they'd moved into this house.

Chuck slowly scrubbed himself, in no hurry to step back out into whatever madness was going on in his bedroom. As soon as he touched his penis, it hardened and lengthened in his hand, an urgent, painful tumescence that Chuck assumed would be wasted. He couldn't believe he'd pulled out of Flavia's mouth to come home to this circus. It served him right. He wondered if it was too late to go back and beg forgiveness. If he took Arrianne to the hospital and talked the doctors into giving her a sedative and letting her stay the night, maybe even keeping her for a few days for psychological evaluation, he'd have all the time in the world to apologize to Flavia.

Then the shower door opened and Arrianne stepped in

89

with lust shining in her eyes like stars and Chuck forgot all about his ex-mistress.

Arrianne still had flecks of vomit on her. Watching her wash it off was oddly erotic, and that was fucking weird. Chuck wasted a few moments considering whether he was the one losing his mind before he began stroking his engorged cock, staring at Arrianne like a kid watching his first porno as she cleaned the yellow and orange streaks from between her breasts. He wasn't doing it for long before she replaced his hand with hers, soaping up his cock and rubbing the head with her slippery fingers. She gripped the base of his cock with one hand and worked it up and down the shaft, jacking him off while rubbing the head faster and faster, bringing him close to orgasm and then slowing down just before he was about to cum, keeping him trembling on the edge of ecstasy.

"I love you, Arrianne," Chuck said as his wife reached up and pinched his nipple hard before taking his cock between her lips, gagging and choking as she slid it farther and farther down her throat, past her tonsils, burying her lips in his pubic hair. He felt his cock throbbing, sheathed in the moist warmth of her esophagus. She grabbed his ass cheeks and pulled him forward, urging him to fuck her throat and Chuck happily obliged. Tears wept from Arrianne's eyes as she gagged on his turgid flesh.

Even as his penis filled his wife's throat, Chuck knew this was not the woman he married. Arrianne had never been a prude, but she'd never been this sexually adventurous, this wanton, this insatiable. The woman gagging on his cock now rivaled Flavia in her oral talents. Whereas just weeks ago, getting head from his wife had felt like an act of mercy, something Arrianne did solely for his benefit, deriving no pleasure from the act and being slightly (though noticeably) disgusted by it. Now she sucked his cock like his semen held the cure for cancer.

There was no way he could ever go back to Flavia. He had no more rationalizations for his infidelity. His wife was now the proverbial whore in the bedroom, lady in company. He had everything he'd ever wanted from a woman. Except she was also probably insane. Right now, with his cock halfway down her throat, her sanity was the furthest thing from his mind. Chuck knew he was an asshole for thinking it, but if insanity made her fuck like this, he wished she'd gone nuts sooner. It was the same way he felt about women who'd been sexually abused as kids. They were always less inhibited in bed, and even while enjoying it, he always felt bad about it, but not bad enough to stop.

For only the second time in their marriage, Arrianne offered her ass to Chuck. He almost climaxed right then just remembering how it had felt the last time, the first time. Tight. Virgin. When she turned around and grabbed her ankles, and then licked her fingers and reached back to insert two of them in her anus, readying it for him, Chuck almost wasted his seed upon the cold ceramic shower tiles instead of his wife's warm, receptive loins.

It didn't take long for Chuck to forget about the strange dog in their bedroom or the even stranger scene of his wife undulating naked and sweating on the bed, gagging while in the midst of some bizarre somnolent pantomime of oral copulation. All he could do was stare in awe at the well-rounded globes of her ass cheeks as he slowly slid his erection in and out of her puckered anus. Arrianne turned her head and looked back at him with eyes smoldering with lust. Impossibly, Chuck felt his erection swell even larger, threatening to tear through his skin.

Then Arrianne eased his cock out of her ass, turned around, and dropped to her knees. She licked the engorged tip of his throbbing erection and smiled up at him. Then she reached back and turned off the shower. "Piss on me, Daddy."

"What?"

"I want you to pee all over me!" She was smiling, having the time of her life, as she begged her husband to urinate on her.

Chuck didn't know what to do. Not only had Arrianne never called him Daddy before, she'd never been into "water sports," golden showers, or whatever the new cool term for urophilia was.

"I—I can't."

"Do it, Daddy. Piss all over me!"

And then it came. A golden stream issuing forth from his swollen cock and spraying Arrianne's face. They were in a shower, she could clean herself up in no time, but that wasn't the point. He was urinating on his beloved wife's beautiful face and was enjoying it. It was turning him on. Arrianne ran her hands over her face, neck, and breasts, washing her flawless alabaster skin in Chuck's urine.

A steady stream of yellow spiraled down the drain. When Chuck finished emptying his bladder, she took his manhood in hand and eased its throbbing length between her lips once again. She stroked and sucked him until he exploded in her mouth. His seed spilled from her lips and dribbled off her chin. Then she pulled him out of her mouth as he continued to cum, coating her face and breasts in a geyser of warm semen. Chuck's legs felt weak as he watched her lick his semen from her lips and use her fingers to scoop it from her chin into her mouth. He had to hold on to the shower door to keep from falling.

"My God! What the hell was that?"

Arrianne didn't respond. She was busy licking Chuck's cum from her fingertips like some extravagant confection, sucking each digit clean while furiously fingering herself with the other hand.

"Vomit on me. Throw up all over me!"

"What? No! I can't do that! That's disgusting!"

Peeing in his wife's face. That was okay, kind of sexy even, but a Roman shower? That was too much. A guy had to draw the line. What was next? Scat?

Arrianne looked wounded. She quickly leapt to her feet and ran out of the shower, snatching a towel on her way out of the bathroom. When Chuck had steadied the quiver in his legs enough to follow, he found his wife back in bed. There were new sheets on the bed and she was cuddling with the old mutt she'd called Dickey and the retriever puppy he'd brought home to surprise her. Her eyes were squeezed shut. Tears glistened in her lashes and leaked from the corners of her eyes, leaving wet trails down her cheeks. Her bottom lip trembled.

"That wasn't me."

Chuck stood in the doorway, not knowing what to say.

"That wasn't me. You know that right? That wasn't me!"

No. The woman who'd asked him to pee on her and then tried to get him to vomit on her bore little resemblance to the demure young lady he'd married. But Chuck liked this woman. She fucked like a porn star, made all his deepest sexual fantasies seem mundane. She put Flavia to shame. He didn't want her to be exorcised or psychoanalyzed away. He liked this wife. He liked her a lot.

CHAPTER ELEVEN
WRATH JAMES WHITE

Arrianne woke slowly to the sound of the new puppy whining to be fed. It was time to walk the dogs. The thought was so normal, something that had been lacking from their lives these last few days. Chuck had been right. They had needed a dog and now they had two.

Dickey walked over and licked her hand. He was putting weight on his injured paw now, though gingerly, lightly testing it for its sturdiness, still not entirely trusting of the wounded limb. Arrianne ruffled his scruffy fur, and Dickey enthusiastically wagged his tail. The puppy scratched at the foot of the bed, jealous.

"Okay, okay. I'm coming."

It was good to have things that needed and relied on her. Chuck was so independent, she sometimes wondered why he even had a wife. He certainly didn't need her—except for sex. In that regard, his need was absolutely voracious. Until recently, she'd had a hard time keeping up with him. Now she wanted to fuck him every time she looked at him. She felt the moistness spread between her thighs as she recalled the feel of Chuck's cock inside her. But Chuck had already left for work. It was just her and the dogs.

"Come on! Time for a walk!"

She pulled on a pair of shorts and a T-shirt, put on a pair of Chuck's tube socks and her running shoes, and then scooped the puppy up in her arms. It took her a moment to find the puppy's leash and put it on. Then she carried it out the front door with Dickey following along at her heels. The second she put the puppy on the ground it began to pee, right on the walkway leading up to the front porch.

"Not a moment too soon," Arrianne said. Dickey wagged his tail in response and Arrianne scratched his back. "You understand me. Don't you, boy?"

He wagged his tail even harder and licked her hand before walking over and lifting his leg to water the rosemary and sage growing along the walkway.

The morning was dreary and gray. Nimbostratus clouds blanketed the sky, threatening rain and hiding the sun, holding the city in perpetual twilight. Arrianne walked along a path through the greenbelt at the end of the block. As she walked, she thought about the house. All her odd behavior had begun the day they moved in. *Perhaps the house is haunted?*

Once entertained, the thought took on increasing weight, the weight of truth. The sales agent had denied that anyone had died in the house, and they had taken the agent at her word. They were so happy to get such a great deal they hadn't thought to question it further. Stupid. It was time she did her own research. Something was definitely not right at Sixty-Five Stirrup Iron Road, and now that she thought about it, they'd only asked whether or not the former owner had died in it, they hadn't asked whether anyone else had.

Arrianne cut the walk short and hurried home to get back to the computer, hoping she wouldn't find anything gross on it when she booted up, but even that was beginning to feel like a normal part of her day. Wake up, cook breakfast, see Chuck off to work, watch bums fucking and puking on each other.

The puppy still didn't have a name. She opened the front door and let both dogs back in the house. Dickey was holding his paw close to his chest again. She had to get him to the vet and get that leg checked out. First the puppy needed a name. *Lucy.* The thought entered her mind like a voice, whispered between her thoughts.

"Here, Lucy!"

The puppy wagged her tail and jumped up on Arrianne's legs.

"Lucy it is then. Let's go see what's on the computer, okay?"

Arrianne felt her stomach tighten as she walked into the study. The screen saver was on. Soap bubbles bounced harmlessly across the screen. Arrianne moved the mouse.

Predictably, the screen came to life with the image of a platinum blonde with breasts larger than her head, wearing garish showgirl makeup and nothing else, being sodomized by a llama. A fucking llama.

It looked like it was killing her. The woman's anus was distended to the circumference of a soda can. She tried valiantly to smile through the pain, repeatedly glancing off camera, obviously taking cues from the director or cameraman or both. She imagined she could hear their voices. "Smile. Act like you're enjoying yourself. Stop grimacing! You're ruining my masterpiece!"

The llama ejaculated deep in the woman's loins and abruptly withdrew. A steady flood of semen poured from the woman's vandalized rectum like melted vanilla ice cream, and a woman who looked like she'd been sleeping under a bridge for weeks was shoved into the frame by someone off camera. A hand, presumably the cameraman's, forced the disheveled woman's face between the blonde's ass-cheeks, where she dutifully lapped at the waterfall of llama sperm gushing from the big-titted whore's well-traveled asshole.

Arrianne stared at the screen for several long seconds before hitting the escape button and closing the website.

Licking llama cum from a woman's asshole? What the fuck is wrong with people?

She typed "Sixty-Five Stirrup Iron Road" into the web browser and got more than a thousand matches. Her dream house apparently had a long and sordid history. The reports of rapes and murders in and around her new home went back more than eighty years. The most recent was a man named Samuel Forrestal. A news article said he'd been "mutilated and dismembered." His sister, Nicci Forrestal, a convicted prostitute and drug addict, had been found at the scene, covered in her brother's blood and raving about vomit and sodomy. That was a little too familiar. Nicci had been suspected of the crime until the medical examiner confirmed it would have taken massive upper-body strength to wrench Forrestal's limbs from their sockets and literally tear the flesh from his bones. The frail, slight of frame Nicci Forrestal would have been incapable of such a feat. She was declared innocent but insane and was committed to an asylum. Everyone suspected she's somehow been involved.

The very first murders known to have been committed in the house were perpetrated by the couple who'd built the place, Harold and Lucy Pearson. Lucy had been half the age of her wealthy husband, a barrel-chested man, well over six feet, with a handlebar moustache. He was said to have been fond of wearing bowties and a black bowler hat and was renowned for his tireless work ethic and remarkable strength. There were rumors that he could lift two bales of hay at once, one in each arm, and carry them for hundreds of yards. Even after making a success of himself in banking, he never shied away from manual labor and was said to have worked every morning on the small farm attached to his house, which at that time sat on ten acres, before heading off to the bank. When he married his young bride, she was no older than seventeen while he was already in his mid thirties and experienced in the ways of the world. They had not even celebrated their third anniversary when she'd begun sneaking out of the house to carouse in the local red-light district.

Reports from witnesses claimed that she drank and smoked and gave herself to men and women alike, including Negroes, Chinamen, and even the Irish! She was spotted on South Street on numerous occasions. Then, South Street was an open-air sex market where sailors, railroad and dock workers, hobos, and other denizens of skid row had relations with prostitutes in dark alleys and beneath the pier. In the weeks before her husband's murder, she was said to have frequented the Dragon Den, a brothel and opium den run by the Chinese mafia that catered to the sexually deviant. There were even rumors that she'd started working there, selling her body to strangers for the sheer thrill of being used and abused by men whose extreme perversions excluded them from the normal whorehouses.

Lucy cavorted openly with the dregs of society, ostensibly to embarrass her husband, who she made no secret of loathing, but also to quench what was rumored to be a ravenous sexual appetite. She was described, by the psychiatrists who later examined her, as a wanton nymphomaniac. When she infected Harold with a case of syphilis, he beat her terribly and locked her in a chastity belt. That's when Lucy had reportedly begun to poison her husband with mushrooms she'd foraged from the woods near their home.

Over the course of several days, according to the news report, Lucy fed her poor husband poison mushrooms ground up in his food and even steeped in his tea. He died in terrific agony as his liver and kidneys shut down. It took him several tortuous days to finally expire. While she was poisoning him, Lucy kept her dying husband locked up in the attic and brought one of her lovers into their home to free her from the chastity belt and keep her company on her death watch. The coroner confirmed that Lucy had begun torturing her dying husband as he lay helpless. There were rope burns around his wrists and ankles from where she'd restrained him while she burned him with hydrochloric acid. There were burns over 60 percent of his body when his corpse was finally discovered, stuffed in a trunk in the attic.

It was believed that Harold Pearson had managed one last act of vigor before finally succumbing to the amatoxin in the mushrooms, during which he'd escaped his bonds and taken his revenge on his wife's lover, tearing him limb from limb with his bare hands. The mutilated corpse of Lucy's lover had been found torn apart in Harold's den just one day before Harold Pearson's own body was discovered.

The paper described Lucy's lover as a local quadroon named Livingston Rousseau who was of mixed French and Negro blood. He was described as a comely young mulatto who had been known to woo white women and had been accused of pandering and prostitution. Lucy was believed to have made his acquaintance at one of the brothels she'd been known to frequent. Several local houses of ill repute catered to whites who preferred their meat dark or slightly tan. Livingston was reported to have moved into the Pearson house after Lucy's husband had been so incapacitated by repeated poisoning that he couldn't protest. They had kept

Lucy's husband locked in a room in the attic, leaving him there to die while they fornicated freely in the man's house, soiling the marital bed with sin. Mr. Pearson must have escaped his attic prison and discovered them in the act when he flew into a murderous fury and tore the man apart.

Arrianne shuddered. Lucy was the name of the woman who had built the house, and Lucy was the name that had come to her when she was trying to think of a name for the puppy. Lucy had been a nymphomaniac, fornicating with bums and hobos, just like the women in the websites that kept popping up on her computer. The last article about Lucy Pearson talked about her trial and subsequent death sentence, and then there was a mention that her sentence had been overturned on appeal and she was found "Not guilty by reason of insanity" and was committed to an asylum. After being locked up for two decades, she was pronounced cured and released. After being let go, she made her way back to the house where she'd murdered her husband. There she took her own life. Journalists were uncharacteristically vague on the details, but it apparently involved some sort of sexual act.

Arrianne scanned through several more newspaper reports about Lucy and Harold Pearson before stumbling upon something that caught her attention. Someone was auctioning off what they claimed was the diary of Lucy Pearson. Arrianne had to have it. It might help explain what—or "who"—had possessed her as she was beginning to suspect Lucy Pearson was not yet done getting her jollies and had been using Arrianne's body to do it. Arrianne clicked on the auction site and put in a bid. She watched the site for most of the day, increasing her bid whenever anyone bid against her. The bidding was at $300 when she finally won. She hoped it was worth it, but she'd been prepared to go up to a thousand if she had to.

By the time Arrianne finished bidding on the diary, Dickey and Lucy were sitting beside her, whimpering and whining. They were hungry and probably needed to go out again. Arrianne was happy to get out of the house. Something in that house smelled terrible. Besides, she needed to buy some dog food and didn't want to be home when Chuck returned from work. She didn't trust herself around him. There was no time for a repeat of last night. Getting that diary had become her most urgent priority. She had told the owner that she would pick it up herself. He only lived in the next county, an hour's drive, and the mail would have taken two days. She couldn't wait that long. A road trip might even help clear her head. Or so she hoped.

CHAPTER TWELVE
WRATH JAMES WHITE
AND RYAN HARDING

It had taken Arrianne less than an hour to reach the home of Wally Ochse. Wally's "home" was a double-wide trailer that looked like it had barely survived the last tornado that whipped through town. The roof had been torn off and replaced with several sheets of corrugated metal. The wheels were gone. It sat directly on the ground, embedded in several inches of mud.

A fence surrounded the trailer, and between the fence and Wally's home was a maze of what could only be described as junk: broken Barbies, baby dolls, and weather-beaten, sun-bleached teddy bears; rusted bikes and automobile parts; broken furniture and cabinets; and appliances of all sorts, including old washing machines, dishwashers, gas ranges, televisions, stereo equipment, and old computers littered Wally's front yard.

Arrianne wondered if she had the right place. A skinny, wrinkled, pockmarked man in his early forties wearing a shoulder-length mullet, cut-off jeans that were frayed at the ends, flip-flops, and a wife beater with mustard stains on it stepped out of the trailer and met her at her car. From the backseat, Dickey snarled as the man approached.

"It's okay, boy. It's okay." Arrianne rubbed Dickey's head and allowed him to lick her face before opening the door and stepping out.

"Wally. Wally Ochse. You Aryan?"

"Arrianne."

"Ain't that what I said? Aryan?"

"Yeah, Aryan. Close enough. Look, not to be rude, but I'm in a bit of a hurry. Can I get the diary please?"

Wally spit a dank stream of brown tobacco and saliva onto an old piss-stained sofa and held out his hand. Arrianne smiled and turned her head away like she was looking for something behind her, trying to politely ignore his outstretched hand for fear of catching something from it that soap and water couldn't remove.

"If you don't want to be rude, then don't be. What's your hurry? Can't wait to get home and bump uglies with the hubby?"

Arrianne didn't know what "bump uglies" meant and didn't have to. Wally punctuated the statement with a few pelvic thrusts to illustrate the colorful colloquialism. He leered at her openly, staring at her breasts like he was waiting for her to whip one out and offer it to him. Lately, it felt like everyone she met either wanted to fuck her or hurt her or both. She'd heard women say that before but had never felt it until recently. Now it awakened all her feminist ire, and it was a struggle to keep it in check. She had to remind herself that she was in the middle of nowhere with a strange man and that Chuck, or anyone else for that matter, didn't have the slightest clue where she was. If things got ugly, she was on her own and would be for a very long time.

"Do you have the diary?"

"I got it, but you ain't paid me yet. I only take cash ... unless you got something you want to trade?" His gaze crawled over every inch of her skin like a bath full of leeches.

Arrianne quickly reached into her purse and pulled out her wallet. She withdrew exactly $300 she'd gotten from the ATM prior to leaving the city. "I brought cash."

He reached for the money but she snatched it away and shoved it back in her purse. "The diary, if you don't mind."

Wally smiled, and his teeth looked like he'd been subsisting on a diet of nothing but candy and meth for the last ten years, which was probably not far from the truth. His dental work had been torn up. The few teeth that remained, clinging stubbornly to his bleeding gums, had blackening holes in them the size of bullet wounds.

Arrianne wondered if this was the type of man Lucy would have spread her legs for. The thought made her stomach threaten to revolt.

Wally pulled his lips back together, thankfully hiding that

102

orthodontic necropolis he called a mouth. "I got your diary. You stay right here, 'kay?"

"I came all the way out here, didn't I? I'm not going anywhere."

The words came out harsher than she'd intended. Wally glared at her, eyes narrowed, obviously not accustomed to having women sass him. He looked like he wanted to hit her, which would have likely led to much worse. Sometimes being an attractive woman was a severe disadvantage. Arrianne tried to discreetly fish in her purse for her pepper spray. There was a pistol in her glove compartment, but that seemed a mile away, and as brave as Dickey was, she didn't think the old dog would be much help to her if Wally started getting frisky.

Wally looked past her into the car, presumably to assess the degree of threat. He scoffed when he saw the old dog with the injured limb and the little puppy wagging its tail and yapping excitedly. Then Wally looked at the money gripped in Arrianne's hand and that seemed to convince him to let the comment slide.

"Be right back. Ya hear?"

"I hear."

He walked back through that labyrinth of junk and into his trailer, leaving Arrianne alone just long enough to take the gun from the glove compartment, check to make sure all cylinders were loaded, and transfer it to her purse. The bulge was noticeable, but she didn't care. Maybe the outline of the Remington .357 would be enough of a deterrent.

Dickey and Lucy began barking and snarling as Wally came back out carrying an old, leather-bound book encased in a clear plastic slipcase. He obviously took care of things he thought might make him a profit far better than he did his own abode.

"Here you go; that crazy bitch's memoirs. Enjoy."

She turned it in her hands and looked at the name stamped into the leather. *Lucy.* "Do you mind my asking where you found this diary?"

"The Pearson family still lived here up until 'bout four or five years ago. They didn't live in that house though. No

Pearson done lived there since the seventies. Not since the last Pearson murder. Way back, his crazy niece, Margaret Pearson, murdered old man Pearson with poison mushrooms just like Lucy did in this here diary. I hear she used to whore around with niggers and kikes just like Lucy too. Naw, they built themselves another big mansion clear across town and rented out the old Pearson place to whoever was stupid enough to pay to live there. Then the Depression came and those rich assholes lost everything, had to sell it all and move. They had a big estate sale. I went up there out of curiosity, but they had everything priced so high like it was some fancy furniture boutique or something instead of a goddamn garage sale. I couldn't afford none of their fancy furniture. But I saw this here diary and I … purchased it."

He grinned again, and this time Arrianne smelled the rot wafting out of Wally's open pie-hole. It made her eyes water. She somehow doubted the man had purchased the diary. The Pearsons would have been smart enough to know what something like this was worth, and if they had everything else priced high and were desperate for money, they would have auctioned it off to collectors. Wally had probably gone to that estate sale and grabbed the one thing small enough to fit under his shirt.

"You mind if I open it?"

"Sure. Go ahead. I ain't no liar. It's her diary all right."

"I'm sure it is. I just want to check its condition," Arrianne lied. She didn't trust Wally as far as she could smell the man.

Arrianne slipped off the plastic book cover and opened the diary to the first page. The handwriting inside was so neat it almost looked like calligraphy. It began with an entry from 1935.

Dear Diary,
What drudgery my life has become! Why did I ever marry this oppressive bore? He would have me spend my days among the gardens or in the house, ordering the servants about until day's end. I should have defied my father and gone to university in Cambridge like other modern women. Now I am a slave to domesticity. My one joy is the freedom to read. I

have discovered some positively scandalous French literature and have been devouring it in my spare time. At night, when my brutish husband takes me to bed, I try to pretend that he is a count or an abbey from one of de Sade's tales, but the unimaginative lout refuses to play along. He is tired all the time and just wants to spill his seed in me as quickly as possible and shuffle off to bed. I cannot stand this!

Jackpot. There was little doubt in Arrianne's mind that this was indeed Lucy Pearson's diary. The language seemed old—more akin to something from 1830 rather than 1930's America, but she supposed that was just a stylistic flourish. She skipped ahead to the middle of the book and read an entry dated April 10, 1936.

Dear Diary,
I have made a scandal of myself! Even the Marquis de Sade could not imagine worse than the deeds I have done in the darkest slums of this decrepit city. Last night, a strange man saw me wandering around South Street and offered me $100 to urinate on my naked flesh. Imagine such a thing! Luckily, Livingston was nearby to protect me had things gotten out of sorts, because I just had to try this new perversion. I have become a bit of a connoisseur of deviancy, and although I have read of these "golden showers," I had never before met anyone acquainted with the act. I agreed and Livingston stood guard at the mouth of the alleyway while I disrobed. I gave my guardian the hundred dollars. I am no common lady of the evening. I don't do this sort of thing for the currency. That all goes to my handsome protector for his services. It is the sheer experience I crave!

"Uh, you done? Can I have my money now?"
Arrianne's face flushed. She looked up from the book and saw Wally staring at her, licking his lips, one hand cupping his testicles through his tight shorts. With the other, he wiped a line of drool from the corner of his mouth after spitting tobacco onto a dandelion that had managed to find one unoccupied spot in which to grow.

"Sure … uh … sorry."

"No problem. Pretty interestin' stuff ain't it? No need to be
'barrassed about it. I done spanked it a few times readin' some
of the things in that book. Though some of that stuff would put
you off your feed. That woman was plain disgustin' with some
of the mess she was into."

Feeling mortified, Arrianne handed Wally the money. He
counted it and shook his head as he stuffed the bills in the
pocket of his cut-off jeans.

Arrianne turned to leave, but Wally was intent on
continuing the conversation. "I tell you, there's some sick shit
in that book for sure, but if you're into that sort of thing, I am
always willing to oblige a beautiful young lady."

Arrianne scowled and recoiled. "No thank you!" She
fumbled for the car door handle, opened it, and slipped in
behind the wheel, slamming the door and quickly locking it.
She heard Wally laughing at her as she started the engine.

"You must be one sick bitch to want to read that diary!
You come back and see ol' Wally if you start to get the itch!"

Arrianne whipped a U-turn and gunned the accelerator,
racing away from Wally and his nauseating breath.

She couldn't wait to get home and read the rest of the
diary. She had an irrational fear that something would stop her,
though, something that didn't want her to discover anything
about the past. She almost expected to see Wally running after
her like the T-1000 in the *Terminator* sequel, but the rear-view
thankfully showed him to be navigating his labyrinth of junk
back to the trailer, probably with the intent to play with his
own junk once inside.

"Pig," she muttered. The nerve of such a degenerate saying
she was the sick one.

Then she thought about the menagerie of perversities
from last night—her "dream," according to Chuck—and how
she'd asked him to vomit on her in the shower. Her shoulders
slumped. He'd clearly been disgusted, probably a mirror of
how she'd looked at Wally just now.

"It wasn't me," she said. It seemed to have more power
said aloud. "It was *her.* Lucy."

The puppy yipped in the backseat.

"Not you." She reached a hand back and put her fingers through the slots in the crate to let the puppy lick her, rubbing the tiny head and ears.

On the passenger seat, Dickey leaned his head out into the rushing wind. Drool splattered across the passenger window of the backseat. Arrianne had an instant flashback to the website of the girls lapping up dog drool. She winced, hoping she wouldn't throw up.

No, that's not my style. Apparently I prefer to have people do it on me these days than actually do it myself.

She had bad luck with the stop lights on her way out of town and kept getting caught by red, so she'd read snippets of the diary as she waited for green. Something from May 1935:

Dear Diary,

I've all but exhausted my reservoir of the French literature and have taken to rereading it in the absence of anything new to excite me. The nation as a whole must seem utterly mad to everyone else. I fear for any country that attempts to engage them in war! The books describe a world I desire, a world where pleasure is there to be taken and the pathetic teachings of religion are mocked and defied in the pursuit of carnality. My ignorant husband believes his god is hiding under our marital bed, ready to sentence him to hellfire if his seed should ever be ejaculated anywhere outside of my cunt. I humiliated him last night by taking him into my mouth and swallowing his climax. His protests were noticeably weak until after he'd spent himself, and then came the guilt. It would be amusing were it not so contemptible. He'll probably give half his savings to his church to pay off his sin.

August 1936:

Dear Diary,

Those with the means to live comfortably are likely to turn to pursuits that would horrify the layman, and those who have plummeted to the bottom of social standing will do anything *to meet their basic needs. I find this endlessly fascinating and useful when the two converge. The sensation, the experiences in my life are everything. It is a life far beyond the blind servitude of sheep who follow the outdated rules of their book of lies and hope that their wasted existence will be rewarded in the afterlife. What fun it shall be, I'm sure, this eternity, with the whole of judgmental charlatans and hypocrites living in the clouds. How I would love to vomit on the clergymen who call upon my husband and waste many of our evenings at home with their holy madness, as if the hours squandered on Sunday aren't punishment enough. How it would disgust them all! Perhaps there's something to be done with this concept of vomit in the slums ...*

Again, August 1936:

Dear Diary,
I continue to sink lower into the very depths of sexual degradation, but I fear that the heightened pleasures I once enjoyed from my transgressions have begun to recede. What is there after this? I know there must be something.

The stop lights ran out after that and she pushed the diary into the glove compartment to make sure Dickey didn't get hold of it while she drove. She'd be home in forty-five minutes. Her excitement to read the rest of Lucy's diary and hopefully learn more to support her possession premise was balanced by the thought of the inevitable scene with Chuck. She'd already imagined the conversation several different ways during the drive out here, and none of them ended with him buying into her theory for a second. No, he'd say she was insane and needed professional help, threaten to divorce her, or ask why they were wasting time with this dumb fantasy when he could be spreading her ass cheeks and sliding into home base. Probably some combination thereof. She knew how impossible it sounded, but what was the alternative? That she had suddenly taken to blacking out and surfing the Internet for bum porn with an emphasis on puke fetishism?

That seemed farther-fetched than possibly being possessed in a house with a colorful history of depravity and violence. Of course no insane person ever truly believes there's something wrong with her, right?

I'm not like that. I'm not.

She felt much more like herself this far from home. The exchange with Wally had been unpleasant, but just to have gotten so many miles away from the house had enormously improved her disposition. But it occurred to her that maybe it was something more.

Maybe it can't reach me out here. Maybe whatever it is has no influence this far away from the house.

She had to go back now though. She'd never convince Chuck they should leave, and if Lucy really was influencing her, would she even still *want* to leave when she got back? Her biggest problem might be finding someone who wouldn't bat an eyelash at the thought of expelling bodily fluids all over her naked body, the more disgusting the better. Even that might not present much of a quandary, she realized.

I was hoping maybe ... I guess ... I wanted you to watch me touch myself.

That pervert at the bar had said that. Had he been embarrassed by the blatant perversity of his own request, or was the awkwardness something else?

She shook her head. She couldn't start seeing a conspiracy in everything strange that had happened to her recently, or she'd start obsessing over Freemason rituals and the grassy knoll at Dealey Plaza. So she'd gone to a bar and some creep had offered her $50 to watch him beat off. It probably happened more than she'd ever imagined (and probably for offers of much cheaper compensation).

Arrianne disappeared into her thoughts, driving on autopilot for the next thirty minutes. She wasn't aware of the changes in her mind the closer she got to home, as slight and gradual as the movement of the minute hand on a clock. Like a clear stretch of road where tendrils of fog unfolded until they became a mobile smokescreen, she couldn't think about anything miles down the road, only the few visible yards ahead of her. Chuck, the house, the diary mattered to her about as much as some play she'd read back in high school.

What did matter, however, was the hitchhiker who stood at the interstate exit.

Ordinarily she would never have even given him a second glance. She'd heard too many horror news stories and friend-of-a-friend cautionary tales that all seemed to feature "raped repeatedly" and ended with "never found her head" to ever entertain the idea of giving a ride to a stranger. Such vagabonds were everywhere back in the city; in fact, they seemed to make up the majority of the population. It became an art form not to see them even if you were feeling gracious enough to toss them a few coins, as though to acknowledge them would guarantee you a spot in a cardboard box one day through some kind of economical contagion. You were safe if you simply didn't *look*.

So why was she not only looking but pulling on to the shoulder to come to a complete stop?

He cocked an eyebrow, as though he couldn't believe she was doing it either. His eyes were bloodshot and a little too wide open, affecting a sort of calm madness that wouldn't have been out of place on a man leading a doomsday cult to mass suicide. His beard looked like some kind of living creature on his face, tufts of it sticking out every which way. Any movement of his head seemed like the creature was shifting position, about to chew his face off. She bet it would feel like a Brillo pad. The hair on his scalp looked equally unruly, dried out and surely uncombed since *Lost* was still on the air. He wore a battered fatigue jacket with bold letters on the breast pocket that had become an unreadable smear. His blue jeans could have fetched a ridiculous price at a vintage store with the appearance of being several years old, including the built-in wear and tear, except his would undoubtedly be the real deal. The knee on one side was held together by fading strands, the knee of the other covered in an honest-to-God patch. She hadn't seen one of those since she didn't know how long. Beside his battered boots sat a duffel bag the color of his jacket, weather-beaten but intact and probably the newest thing he had, something that might have been fairly young when there was still an East and West Germany.

That's probably where he keeps the heads.

Lastly, he cradled a pathetic cardboard sign, the flap torn unevenly from a box. PLEZE HELP. She imagined he didn't have many takers with such a vague request. Not WILL WORK FOR FOOD, not even WILL PUKE ON CAMERA FOR SICK THRILLZ, just PLEZE HELP. She found that sad.

Dickey pulled back from the window and looked at her inquisitively, whining. *We're not really giving this psycho a ride, are we?*

"Afraid so," she said, scratching behind his ears. She patted the backseat beside Lucy's crate and gave him a little push, and Dickey reluctantly limped back to it between the passenger and driver seats. She then pushed open the passenger door toward the hitchhiker—

He's not a hitchhiker, he's a bum, *a* hobo, *a* vagrant.

—to let him in.

He hoisted his duffel bag onto the floorboards and climbed into the car. Something bounced off his fatigue jacket when he did. Dog tags. She examined all the gray in his hair and his beard and pegged him in his mid- to late-sixties. If he hadn't combed his hair since *Lost* was on the air, he probably hadn't taken a true shower since the characters got into the hatch. Her eyes watered and she had to swallow down bile as his unwashed odor filtered through the vehicle like a poisonous gas leak.

She smiled at him like she didn't notice. It was easy enough. She *liked* it. The heat that had been simmering between her thighs even as she'd pulled to the side now threatened to boil over at his proximity and its mephitic bouquet. Her wetness had saturated the crotch of her panties.

He'd probably eat them whether or not they were edible panties.

She opened her mouth to say something, and until she actually heard the words, she wasn't completely sure she wasn't about to offer *him* fifty bucks to watch her bring herself to a climax right where they sat.

"Where are you going to?"

He hunched in the seat like a prison inmate over a tray, hoping to not be noticed and stabbed in the lung with a shank. He twisted his head to look at her, his eyes watery. "To hell, probably," he said simply. He stared back into his lap. A hand floated up to clench around his dog tags.

Arrianne waited for more, but he didn't offer it. "Can I … drop you anywhere on the way?"

Somewhere deep within her was a voice sounding an alarm at this predicament she had willingly placed herself, but it was so faint as to be merely an enhancement to the excitement. It might have been a lot louder even a few miles ago, though probably unnecessary altogether since she would have reacted with disbelief to be told she would pick up a (*bum, hobo, vagrant*) hitchhiker. Not now, though. Now that voice was like the whisper of a ghost on a tape recording.

"Wherever," he said. He looked back at Dickey, who panted a bit more animatedly. "I ate a dog in Vietnam," he announced. "This one knows it."

Arrianne checked the rear-view. If that was Dickey's "you ate one of my kind" look, then apparently the trees in the woods and the weatherman on TV had also eaten dog.

"There's things coming for me," he continued. "Awful creatures. You can barely see their eyes. Always watching." He held a hand out in front of him and made a beckoning gesture with his fingers. "*Come home.*"

Arrianne didn't have the faintest idea how to respond to anything he'd said so far. She put the car in drive and eased back onto the ramp. "Some weather we're having, isn't it?" she said. "I'm—" Who was she, indeed? She wasn't about to give him her real name. "Lucy." Her smile never faltered.

"Brad," he grunted. "Brad Zeller."

"A pleasure to meet you, Brad. You been waiting out here long?"

He shrugged. "Couldn't really say. I've seen the skin rot off a head before. It was like time-lapse photography. Could have been minutes or hours. Could have been days. I never moved. It was like being in a snow globe, but no snow. Just a head. Rotting on a spike."

"Well, that's certainly … exciting. Was this in Vietnam?"

He flinched slightly and cupped a hand to his mouth. She heard a wet jostling sound as he put his fingers through his lips to straighten something out. Once he seemed assured that everything was settled, he answered her. "That wasn't nothing compared to what I saw out in Vietnam. That's why I'm going to hell, you understand." He pronounced *Vietnam* so that it rhymed with "dam."

"Like what?" she asked. The panicked whisper begged her not to provoke him, but the need to provoke *herself* was far greater, rapturous. "What was it like, all that death and despair?"

"Like …" He choked for a moment and hawked up something that he proceeded to gulp back down with an effort. "Like breathing. You go insane at first. You're seeing bodies when you close your eyes. Then it's kind of cool. You realize you can do any fucking thing you want to. You're like Double-Oh Seven, but you don't got an exploding pen or a trick car or nothing. What you got is some Claymores and an M-16, and you're going around cutting off ears for a necklace. It's power." He smiled faintly and then grimaced. "But then one day it's like breathing. You do it every day without even thinking about it."

Breathing. She was doing that faster now herself, exhaling through her mouth. She squirmed in her seat where things felt gloriously wet, hotter with his casual disregard for both killing and bathing alike. She kept one hand on the wheel, but the other crept over to her left breast, cupped and pinched the nipple through her bra. She hadn't considered not wearing one without knowing who'd be selling her the diary. It had definitely felt like the right move at the time, but now she wished she hadn't bothered. She wanted to see her erect nipples poking through her shirt, obvious and unashamed in the least. She squeezed herself roughly, inviting pain and relishing it in a way she never had before she and Chuck moved into that house.

Brad just stared at his folded hands in his lap like a man praying at church, oblivious to her movements.

113

"Tell me about something you saw over there," she invited. "Something awful."

He didn't respond, muttering to himself.

Arrianne's brow furrowed. "Don't hold out on me now, Ben."

"Brad," he corrected.

"I couldn't give a fuck less what it is. Sing for your supper, *Ben,* or I'll stop the car and let those freaks catch up to you."

He looked up sharply from his reverie. It was difficult to say if he was startled given that the bulging eyes seemed to be a permanent feature, but she'd gotten through to him without question.

Then more urban scenery passed them by, about as noticeable as a faded painting in the room of a rundown motel. Arrianne's feet worked the brake and accelerator as needed, almost independently of her mind. She'd slid out of both shoes without realizing it and nudged them out of the way, her toes digging into the thin carpet of the floor mat just for the friction. The polish changed color depending on sunlight. They had been purple at Wally's but were now a light shade of blue. She bit her lip, wondering if she needed to prod him again with another threat about kicking him out, but he finally rewarded her request.

"We were at this village. Seemed like we always found them the day after we'd seen some action too. Some of them were in with the North. Had to be. That close to the shit, man, no doubt about it. But the gooks, they'd just look at us like we had a dick growing out of our forehead. 'No, GI, we not VC.' The hell they weren't. We had two or three guys from the platoon in body bags, and we just decided the next village was VC even if they were wearing Stars and Stripes underwear and using Ho Chi Minh photos to wipe their ass. Had 'em all dragged out of the huts, several of them in a line. A bunch of mama-sans were leading the chorus, the usual shit, swearing up and down they no VC. Fuckin' Hodson, he's got like a billion-yard stare in his eyes and more importantly an M2 flamethrower, and he just opens up on the whole row of those zipperheads. A solid sheet of flame, we're talking a human brushfire of old ladies, husbands and wives, little kids *incinerated.* No young men though. They weren't VC, no way, but the strongest people they coulda had were nowhere to be found … except probably in a tunnel somewhere with an AK-47, a bowl of rice, and a mommy, daddy, and granny *beaucoup* flambéed."

It was the weirdest thing, but Arrianne thought she could even smell the stench of burning death. Perhaps in the throes of her lust it was easy enough to convert the reek of her passenger to that of a smoldering corpse pile. All those people burned up in an instant. She felt light spasms between her legs. Each time she inhaled seemed to bring the massacre closer to her, like a shimmering mirage.

"Less screaming than you'd expect," Brad continued. "When you're completely wrapped in fire like that, your lungs blow out. That's what Doc said. Rice paddies not half a click away, but they didn't have a chance. *Water, water everywhere and not a drop for dinks.* I think Bennett said that and we all laughed. Some of them were still running around like headless chickens and we laughed anyway. Had to put them down if they got too close. They couldn't see where they were going, but they flat picked 'em up and set 'em down in a hurry, like they could get away from it somehow. No dice. Someone puked from the smell of burning hair and flesh. I think it was Cooper. All that fire liquefied the sandals on some of them, like little oil slicks. Charred husks everywhere you looked, probably thirty of them with their fucked-up teeth. Wasn't no Colgate in Agent Orange."

Brad paused to fumble around inside his mouth again, as if the mention of teeth had triggered the impulse. Something seemed to snap into place.

It distracted Arrianne momentarily, agitated her, but he thankfully resumed the narrative.

"Hodson never laughed. When they all stopped moving and were just smoldering out there in the sun, he lit them up *again.* It was miserably hot, but he didn't care. Felt like a hundred twenty degrees. Then Murphy walked out of a hut with a bag in his hand, holding it over his head like a trophy.

We couldn't believe it. Marshmallows. He saw some of those bodies ablaze again and proceeded to stick a marshmallow on a twig and hold it over the flame. One of those mama-sans, I think. He stood there and roasted a marshmallow off her burning corpse. Those scorched bodies were everywhere, and you wouldn't believe the stench. I didn't think I'd ever stop smelling it. I still wake up sometimes thinking it's happening again. Coop puked a second time. We just watched Murphy do it, grinning at us the whole time and eating it like the finest steak ever cooked, but I know we were all thinking the same thing ... where the hell had the gooks gotten those marshmallows?"

He finally looked over at Arrianne as though he hoped he could solve this ageless mystery.

"From the VC?" she suggested.

He nodded. "There it is. We threw a bunch of playing cards on those bodies. One of them—it had to be a kid because it was so small—Murphy slammed a boot right into the chest and it went right through, all the way to the ground. He booted its head clean off. A couple of guys kicked it around, but I didn't. It was way too hot. Someone put a Coke can in what was left of somebody's hands. It looked hilarious. No one had a camera, though."

Brad's face hardened. "Then I came back to the world and a bunch of long-hairs spit on me and called me a baby killer. I never killed no babies. I just watched the other guys do it. Some gratitude for serving, I tell you what."

Arrianne noticed with mild surprise but no concern at all that she did not recognize the area they were in now. It was rural farmlands, and she'd maneuvered them off the main roads. There had been the occasional car in the oncoming lane, but nothing in her own for the last few miles. She'd driven past her turn-off toward Stirrup Iron Road since she had no intention of taking him back home. A shame because he probably had several more hot stories like this one. It could be like *1001 Arabian Nights,* albeit with more corpses and carnage.

Still, she had to ask, "If all that killing was just like

breathing, why are you so worried about hell?"

He looked at her again, the eyes now brimming with obvious madness again. "*Because* it was like breathing. Because when something like that is normal to you, you're lost *forever*. No, those things want me, all right."

Arrianne pulled over abruptly. There was only the merest shoulder on this stretch of road, and most of the car dipped down into the slope of land beside the asphalt. She put it in park, freed her seat belt from the clasp, and swiveled to face him. "They're not the only ones who want you, Ben."

"My name is—"

"Shut the fuck up. Let me talk."

There shouldn't have been any shift in the balance of power. He was a former soldier, a killer who was quite possibly psychotic. Her fearlessness seemed to take him aback, though, as if he recognized one of his own. He stared back at his folded hands again.

"Look at me, Ben."

He lifted his head and turned it to her very slowly, as though a knife had been plunged into the side of his neck.

"I liked your story. It got me extremely hot, and I am sitting in a *puddle* right now. You reek like someone's asshole baked in an oven, and I keep thinking I'm going to throw up from the godforsaken *stench* from you, but I like it and it turns me on. Do you understand that?"

He nodded almost imperceptibly, clearly *not* understanding.

"Sure you don't. It doesn't matter. Riddle me this, though, Ben … what was the prettiest pussy you ever saw in your life? A girl in *Playboy*? A high school sweetheart?" She smiled cruelly as a thought occurred to her. "Your mama's?"

She saw a sliver of his tongue as he licked his lips through the mesh of his beard. "It was … immaculate," he said with true reverence. His eyes glazed over. He looked directly at her without seeing her anymore. "Fuzz barely thicker than a peach. The lips were like the petals off a tulip. It was perfect in every way, planted between the smoothest thighs." He smiled warmly at the memory.

"And who was she, Ben?"

He shrugged. "Hell if I know, ma'am. Just some gook girl who tripped a Claymore. Blew her into a good five fuckin' pieces and shredded that sackcloth thing she was wearing into another thousand. The knees up to the waist were okay. Her guts were strewn from her waist to her torso for a good three yards, but all I saw was that amazing cunt. No one had a camera that day, either. Damn the luck."

The image should have repulsed her. She understood this, but only in the most rudimentary fashion. Mostly there was just the thrill of the forbidden. Even so, she needed a slightly different tack. "And what about when you actually crammed your rock-hard dick into a girl's pussy, Ben? What was the most spectacular of them all? The one you still sometimes dream about and wake up with about a pint of cum in your shorts?"

"Well, I'd have to say it was that same girl, ma'am. Like I said, the knees to the waist were okay, and a couple of us took a turn. Coop puked over *that* too, but he went third. I went after him. I think I'd have blasted the top of her skull apart if it had all still been attached. I came like a mortar shell. That was probably my best day in 'Nam, when you get down to it."

"You ... you screwed the lower half of that girl's body?" God, that was so *hot.* Her thighs rubbed together as she ground her ass into the seat, nudging her sex against the cushion, massaging.

"Well, yeah. And the head too. Hodson went first cuz it was his Claymore, so he got dibs, but it was taking him *forever.* We were trying to pass the time, and then Murphy goes, 'Hey, look what I found.' It was the head and neck, of course. So the rest of us got down to brass tacks with passing it around and humping it. Doc claimed by the third dick that our loads were dripping out of the neck like an IV, but I didn't see—"

Arrianne touched a finger to his lips to shush him, harder than she'd intended. Something jostled loose. The top row of his teeth slipped through his lips. She caught it in her palm before he could snatch them. She smacked his hand. "All good things to those who wait, soldier boy. And if you haven't had anything to compare to that girl all those years ago, you've waited *way* too long."

She unbuttoned her capris and slid them down her thighs, never relinquishing the row of his false teeth. She slid her right leg completely out . She had maneuvered herself so that her back faced the driver's side door, her right leg bent with the knee prodding the back of her seat and the left as apart from it as the steering wheel and console would allow.

The bulge of Brad's eyes now expressed as much surprise as lunacy. He raptly stared between her thighs at the beige crotch of her panties, like it was some sort of vortex funneling him down into oblivion and a complete loss of self. She glanced down. No, they weren't see-through from her wetness but soaked all the same. She curled her fingers beneath the fabric at her thigh and yanked them to the side. She felt even hotter with the underwear pulled away.

"Isn't this so much better than some pathetic dead girl's quim? *Wet* and *alive*, instead of cold and rotting?"

He may have nodded, but it was difficult to say; he was transfixed. The puppy stood on her hind legs in the backseat, forepaws on the crate, yipping, and Dickey barked as though he should get in on the act as well, a sound like a gunshot in the sealed confines of the car. Brad didn't notice at all. His breath came out in labored gasps, like a woman doing Lamaze, a steady stream of halitosis blowing into her nostrils.

Arrianne opened her fingers enough to reveal his teeth. They managed to break through his trance, and he instinctively reached for them.

She clenched her fingers closed again. "Ah-ah-ah," she chided. "I'm not done with them yet. Watch."

The row of teeth effortlessly slid into her vagina, the opening so slick she wouldn't have been surprised if she could have pushed all her fingers inside to the knuckles—maybe her whole hand.

Brad stared in amazement like a kid whose mind had been blown by a disappearing coin trick. It didn't fit snugly with the jagged arch, but the discomfort of the sensation was wonderfully immediate, his look of astonishment empowering.

"God, I need to cum," she said. She slipped her fingers

down between her legs, rubbing her clit in quick circles, knowing exactly how fast and how much pressure she needed. It didn't take long at all, between that and the alien feel of his teeth inside her, his breath a wretched fog blowing hotly into her face. She could picture him gnawing at the guts of road kill, slobbering over it like a starving dog. She cried out inside of a minute, her thighs clenching as the spasms rolled through her. Her head twisted against the window until the waves of pleasure subsided. She exhaled in a long rush, chilled sweat dripping down the back of her neck. Her thighs unclenched. She felt like she could melt into the floorboards.

The teeth now irritated her in the wake of orgasm.

Brad watched attentively as if he expected something else to emerge from the magic box. It was merely his teeth though, glistening like they had been coated in petroleum jelly from her juices. He reached for them, and again she slapped his hand away.

"Open," she said. She pointed to his lips when he gave her a befuddled look.

His lower lip dropped uncertainly, and Arrianne pushed the slippery teeth back into his mouth.

CHAPTER THIRTEEN
RYAN HARDING
AND BRYAN SMITH

Arrianne still wasn't home when Chuck returned.

Thank Christ.

No telling where she'd gone, but she could take her time. He still wasn't sure what he'd say to her about last night. It wasn't something you could just let lie, could you, the elephant in the room?

An elephant desperate to be puked on for sexual gratification.

He winced as he loosened his tie. How does someone even discover a fascination in something like that? Maybe he was better off not knowing. If he saw someone throw up, he was always right there on the verge of joining them. Setting up a vomitorium in the bedroom definitely wasn't Chuck's idea of ball-draining excitement. It was a crying shame, because the *other* stuff was top notch, firing on all dick-sucking and ass-fucking cylinders. Why did she suddenly have to get all weird with him?

He found a hanger for his tie in the closet and slipped the fashion noose on the hook with the others. He kept them all pre-tied so he didn't have to fool with them for minutes at a time. He thought he'd left them behind altogether when he switched to telecommuting, but he still had clients who wanted face-to-face meetings if they were within a reasonable distance. He was grateful for the distraction today. He probably would have invented a meeting just to avoid the house for most of the day. Although it occurred to him that maybe he wouldn't have had to. He'd only returned home the night before and was supposed to be staying away for a few nights.

It was bizarre how she'd lashed out at him when they'd first moved in and she found all those sick sites with the bums on the computer. He now had to accept that she'd just been trying to feel him out on it to see if he'd been into it at all. She'd really sold her disgust, though; she'd have been nominated alongside Meryl Streep if it were a movie. Did she really think he'd say, "Hell, I don't think it's all that bad—it's even kind of hot how he puked in that hefty woman's face and shot his payload into the chunks"? With her level of indignation, he would have agreed with her even if he *hadn't* been sickened by the scene, although he most certainly had been.

She'd even put it on *his* computer. He'd take a sledge hammer to the hard drive now before he'd ever take it to any repair place. Those people undoubtedly saw some crazy porn shit every day, but probably just comparably wholesome stuff like bukkake or some dog-on-girl clips that someone checked out simply because he knew it had to exist online somewhere. The same reason he'd watched *2 Girls 1 Cup*. He didn't think for a minute it would turn him on, but once he knew it was out there, how could he *not* look?

He considered himself fairly vanilla when it came to the bedroom. He'd entertained the thought of anal sex with Arrianne of course, but she'd quickly shot down that possibility with record speed years ago, and he decided he'd just have to nurture that fantasy on his own. He had a couple of pornos stashed away to help out with that. A few volumes of *Analrama* were really all he needed ("Four hours at a whack!" the jumbo boxes proclaimed). A scene here and there on his laptop did the trick. It wasn't like *Twin Peaks* or something with a continuing storyline you had to follow. You just blew your load and hit the bricks.

He went back downstairs and spotted Arrianne's laptop on the living room couch. It was in hibernate mode.

Hey ... I gotta know.

Chuck woke it up. Married couples needed their secrets— he had Flavia and *Analrama*, after all—but all bets were off with this. What if it was even worse than what she'd loaded on his computer? That didn't seem possible, but why would she start him out with the hardest stuff if it was intended to be a gateway drug to puketopia?

She had several tabs of filth open on her browser. He

sighed, now as depressed as he was disgusted. The first was actually kind of tame. It was called *Bum's Rush*. It was a candid camera operation where the "host" paid obviously homeless people to haul down a pretty woman's skirt or rip open her blouse to reveal the goodies beneath and then run for the hills while spy cameras immortalized it all. It was kind of funny how the women reacted, and funnier still when someone with quick reflexes managed to snatch a hobo's sleeve and blast him with pepper spray before he could get away. The host caught as much as he could of that and then surreptitiously evacuated the premises when some concerned bystanders threw the shrieking bum a boot party. That one had the most "likes" of the clips.

The doorbell rang. Chuck felt a spike of panic and had to remind himself he was alone in the house. Arrianne could return any minute though, and with the fourteen missed calls on his phone this afternoon alone, he had a legitimate reason to worry.

Fourteen missed calls, he thought. *I must have had my phone on mute. Dumbass! Please, God, don't let it be Flavia.*

Logically he knew she had no idea where he lived, either before they'd moved to Stirrup Iron Road and now, but he had this nightmare premonition that she'd be waiting for him and only too happy to hang around until Arrianne returned.

As he crept to the door, trying not to make any noise, he had a moment to marvel at the irony of being scared that his wife with a secret double life of emetic erotica would find out that he'd had a very normal affair with a beautiful woman. He checked through the peephole and sighed with relief.

Chuck opened the door to a teenager of high school age on the porch. He was a few inches taller than Chuck, more than six feet. He seemed strong in a wiry way. He wore a T-shirt with a completely unreadable band name. A grin instantly disappeared from the boy's face when he saw Chuck.

Well, screw you too, Junior.

"Yes?" Chuck prompted.

"Uh, hi. My name's Eric. I'm just going around seeing if anyone is looking for help with chores." The smile didn't threaten to reappear. The kid seemed either disappointed or maybe even a little pissed off.

Chuck had already decided the little bastard wouldn't be getting dime one from him. "Sorry, but I think we've got everything covered."

"Look, dude, is your wife here? I'd like to talk to her."

Chuck began to wonder which would truly be worse—a visit from Flavia or an aggravated assault against a minor charge. "Nope, *dude*. Just me, myself, and I. And we're getting along just fine, thanks."

Eric rolled his eyes. "Okay, man, whatever. Just trying to help out."

"You could be a huge help by beating your feet right now," Chuck said. He slammed the door, blocking out the stupid look on the little punk's face.

What the hell's wrong with kids anymore? Lucky I didn't rearrange his face for him.

He hurried back to the couch and the laptop. He didn't want to get busted invading her privacy, and time was of the essence.

The second tab was much less quaint than *Bum's Rush*. The clip was titled *Horseplay*. A grimy woman in tattered clothes masturbated a horse to orgasm while a couple of similarly attired males caught the massive effluvium in a punch bowl. The one to consume the most semen would receive a sleeping bag and a box of wine. The trio began to pass it around, sipping the creamy concoction with notably less enthusiasm as the number of rotations increased. Chuck wondered how they could even keep score with this system. Male Hobo #2 was the first to puke. The woman sank to her knees before the milky puddle to lap it up, evidently on her way to being the big winner.

Chuck clicked out of that one. It was wretched, yet he'd hung in there much longer than he would have believed possible. He knew his wife loved animals, but this was beyond the pale, to say the least. It suddenly seemed awfully sinister that she had taken the dogs with her.

Dickey was humping the air right near my face and my mouth was open. He ejaculated in my mouth!

She'd blamed it on the house. Sure. What else would you

say in that situation? *Yep, Chuck ... it's exactly what you think it is. Sorry, baby.*

Was this what it was like to watch somebody go insane? Had the warning signs been there all along and he'd somehow missed them until she started hitting the real freak milestones?

She needed fucking Prozac or *something* in a bad way.

He planned to put the laptop back to hibernate but then noted something the tab revealed when he'd clicked out of *Horseplay*. The still was of yet another bum, surprise, surprise. There was a telltale brown bottle of cheap alcohol on a table beside him.

The clip was called *Peel Slowly and See.*

Against his better judgment, Chuck clicked play. There was a chair beside the table with the brown bottle. The man staggered around to it. He wore brown corduroy pants with a length of rope for a belt. He untied the knot, and the pants dropped to his ankles. He collapsed into the chair without any semblance of grace, utterly shit-faced. He seized the brown bottle, which he'd already emptied. Chuck jumped when he abruptly shattered the bottle against the table and lifted up his shirt to reveal his penis. The camera drew in closer.

Turn it off, Chuck, he thought, but another part of him argued, *come on, he's not really going to do it.*

Even if he *didn't* do "it," there was no reason to keep watching, but Chuck made no move to stop it.

The bum brought the jagged neck of the bottle to his partially erect organ. He cupped one side with his palm and mashed the bottle into the elongated skin, instantly opening a spurting wound. He sucked in air but did not seem deterred in the least by pain. He grew fully erect. He curved the bottle around to where the neck faced him and pushed it forward. The glass pushed his penis into his belly, slicing a red grin at the base of the member. Then he dragged it up the length of his girth all the way to the head. He cried out with this incision, but it didn't even seem like anguish so much as exquisite pleasure. Blood oozed from the crooked mouth he had created and continued to jet in excited spurts from the first cut on the side.

The color drained from Chuck's face.

It's special effects ... it's gotta be. They made it look like a guy turned into a werewolf in The Howling *twenty-something years ago. A realistic dick execution these days would be child's play. There's probably something like this in one of those Eli Roth movies.*

The bum slightly rotated the neck and carved up his full length right beside the last cut, and then he did it again to the opposite side so now three wounds gushed. The bottle slipped from his fingers and shattered on the floor. He made pincers of his thumb and index finger and lowered them to his mutilated sex. His hand shook with tremors, but he managed to seize the flap of one wound. He tore the skin in a downward motion, opening a deeper cavern of crimson gristle. Now the blood poured out in a stream into the matted fur of his scrotum, with rivulets dripping off the edge of the chair. Arteries continued to pump projectile sprays like a rapid-fire lawn sprinkler. He grabbed a corner near the base of his penis and pulled it up like the address label on a package.

Chuck didn't close the browser—he slammed the laptop shut and bolted up from the couch like it had turned into a rattlesnake.

"Jesus Christ!"

Why would she look at anything like that? Why would *anyone*?

He went to pour himself a drink in the kitchen. His hands shook like the hobo's in the video. He spilled whiskey on the counter.

Doing anything special with the bottle when you're done, Chuckster?

He slammed back the shot and poured another.

Naturally his cell phone vibrated in his pocket at that moment. He checked the screen, momentarily forgetting that he had been dreading this.

Marshall's Gardening calling.

For only the fifteenth time today, in addition to twenty-seven text messages. He'd have enjoyed the constant vibrating of his phone so close to his groin were it not for the ball of acid in his stomach that swished around every time she attempted contact. He'd deleted the voice mails and texts without listening or reading, playing it all very ostrich-like, but Flavia wasn't going away. If she ever discovered his new phone number, he estimated she'd wait approximately twelve seconds before trying to ruin his life. He could get his number changed, but so many clients contacted him that way, and he wasn't sure he had them all saved on his phone or in his e-mails. He'd be potentially throwing away money, not to mention Arrianne would find it suspicious.

If she's still sane enough for things like that.

"Fuck it," he said. He wanted the distraction, needed it even. He hit the talk button. "Yeah?"

"I'm very, *very* disappointed in you, Papa Bear. You've been ducking my calls all day."

"We don't have anything more to say to each other, Flavia. I made that clear."

"But you answered just now, didn't you, baby?"

Chuck drank the other shot and blinked the ensuing tears from his eyes. "Look, it's over, okay? I shouldn't have done any of this and I'm sorry you got hurt."

She laughed. "I'm sure you cried yourself to sleep last night over hurting me."

He decided not to tell her she was the furthest thing from his mind after last night until she'd initiated Operation Barnacle on his phone this afternoon.

"So I guess your wife isn't boring you all of a sudden?" she asked.

"You could say that," he deadpanned.

"She bored *me* just hearing about her. Like you married a Quaker or something."

"I didn't make her out that way at all," he said.

"You said she wasn't interested in sex anymore. And if she ever was, she didn't want your cock anywhere near her mouth."

"But I still love her," he said. *Don't I?* "Besides. Things are different."

"Oh, I'm sure. I'm not stupid, Chuck. You got what you wanted from me, and once you got it you hated me for doing it. Same story with all men."

"I don't h—"

"If I'd let you fuck me in my ass like you hinted, you'd have tried to leave even sooner after you'd got your fill."

"My wife lets me," he said. "She'll do anything now."

And I'm beginning to think literally anything.

"So what if she does? I've seen her picture in your wallet. She's got nothing on me and you know it."

Certainly not your modesty.

"You can't name any flaw for me at all, can you?" she challenged. The tone implied he'd better *not,* but *Peel Slowly and See* was way too close to the front of his memory to not throw down the gauntlet and give it a bigger push to the rear.

"Come on," Chuck said. "You like Busta Kapp, for Christ's sake."

"That's the best you can do?" She laughed like it was absurd, but he could tell he'd really pissed her off. "Lots of people like him. *Bust in Yo' House* was number one on the Billboard charts for three straight weeks! He won a Grammy for 'Skrate Up Thug'! You're the weirdo here, not me."

His bemusement faded. She'd called Arrianne ugly last night and he'd dismissed it as jealous rage, but what she'd said a moment ago was a lot more specific.

"Wait a minute," he said. "What do you mean you saw her picture in my wallet? I never showed you that."

"Oh, you *do* pay attention to what I say. How sweet. No, I got a good look at everything in there when you went to the bathroom without your pants." She was silent for a beat. Then: "Even your new business cards."

Peel Slowly and See suddenly didn't matter to him a bit.

"You know"—he heard the smile in her voice—"the ones with your new address and everything."

"Let's go for a walk, Ben."

The bum gave her a strange look. Okay, so every look he directed at her or anyone else was by default a strange look. The gnarled old son of a bitch had an extra level of strange encoded in his DNA that set him well above the national average. But this time his expression conveyed a degree of wide-eyed perplexity that imbued his oddness with an almost comical quality. He blinked rapidly, and a corner of his mouth twitched a few times. After a few moments of staring at her like a brain-damaged imbecile, he shifted in his seat and craned his head slowly around, taking in the empty stretch of rural road and the densely wooded area beyond the road's shoulder.

He closed a hand around his dog tags, holding on to them like a Catholic woman clutching a strand of rosary beads. The tags did seem to hold a talismanic quality for him, which was none-too-surprising given the likely significance of what they represented in his life. "I done walked a good spell already today. So unless you're kickin' me out, I'm good. Done had enough exercise for one day."

Arrianne smiled and put a hand on his knee. "I don't think you have, Ben."

"Please stop calling me Ben."

She kept her smile in place and dug the tips of her fingers hard into his bony knee, making him wince. "You know what, Ben? I think you're afraid of women. I think you're afraid of me."

Ben grimaced as she again intensified the pressure on his knee, but he said nothing.

Arrianne laughed. "Yes, you're afraid of women. The prettiest pussy you've ever seen was on the bottom half of a blown-to-shit gook bitch. I'll bet that's because hers was just about the only real-live pussy you've ever seen up close and personal." She giggled and relaxed her grip on his knee a notch. The reason for the giggle was two-fold: she was getting an incredible kick from so easily intimidating the confessed mass-killer and corpse-fucker, and because of the massive hard-on tenting the front of his threadbare jeans.

"I'm also willing to bet that gook pussy is still the only pussy you've ever fucked. Isn't that right, Benjamin?"

He let out a breath and clutched his dog tags harder. "You think you know all about me, but you don't know nothin'. Ain't nothin' a man like me has to fear from the likes of you. I got bigger things to worry about."

Arrianne giggled again and pointedly eyed his swollen

crotch. "I don't know, baby, looks like your biggest concern right now is me."

"I'm damned. Got things after me. Shadow lurkers. They taunt me. Toy with me. Laugh when I'm tryin' to sleep. I've spent every day of my life since the 'Nam tryin' to stay one step ahead of 'em. That's why I ain't had time to fuck no women."

Arrianne smirked. "Right. You keep telling yourself that. I know the real truth." She reached across and pulled the door handle, popping open the door on his side. She couldn't help grinning at the way he recoiled from her. "Here's what's happening, Ben. We're going into the woods, deep enough to ensure no one will see or hear us. And then we're gonna take our clothes off and fuck like wild animals."

She grabbed her purse and got out of the car, moving to the shoulder of the road while the bum remained in the shotgun seat and tracked her progress with his googly, twitching eyes. When he still made no move to join her, she pulled the passenger side door fully open and ordered him out in her sternest voice. Her tone made Dickey whimper and elicited some concerned yaps from the pup.

The bum heaved a big sigh and maneuvered his way out of the car. He reached for his duffel bag, but Arrianne slammed the door shut. "Did you just try to ditch me, Ben?"

"My name's Brad. I don't wanna ride with you no more."

Arrianne gripped him by an elbow and steered him toward the line of trees beyond the road's shoulder. "That way, Ben. Into the woods. Walk ahead of me."

He shook his head. "I don't like this."

"I don't care."

He eyed her with palpable suspicion and cast another searching glance up and down the road. "Why ain't there no cars out this way? There should be cars."

She gave him another nudge toward the woods. "Quit stalling. Go."

He shook his head again. "No."

She removed the .357 from her purse and aimed it at his chest. "Yes. Go."

Another tired sigh, followed by another desperate, yearning look at the empty stretch of road. "Shit."

Arrianne laughed. "Story of your life, I'll bet. No one around to look out for you. No one who gives even one little shit. Go."

This time he went.

She followed him into the woods, paying no mind to the louder sounds of canine distress emanating from the car. The dogs would be fine. What she had in mind shouldn't take too long. She maintained a distance of about six feet as she trailed the bum into the woods, keeping the gun aimed at the center of his back. A distant part of herself registered alarm over the dangerous notion that had taken root in her head over the course of her conversation with the damaged old vet. This part of her recognized the impulse as alien. It was a thing she would never contemplate doing in the normal course of things. Hell, it would never even *occur* to her. And if it *had* occurred to her, she would have felt an instant repulsion.

But she wasn't herself right now. That much was evident. Pleasuring herself with the man's slimy old upper-denture plate was only the most extreme aspect of an overall disconnect from her normal, more civilized state of mind. There were more subtle nuances involved. The way she had callously—and repeatedly—referred to the blasted-to-smithereens girl from the bum's tale as a "dead gook bitch," for instance. Such a phrase would normally elicit disgust from her when spoken by another person. She had never been prone to racial slurs, much less in so vile a context.

There could be only one explanation.

Lucy.

It was shocking to think the dead woman's perverse influence extended beyond the house, but the radius of influence seemed quite wide. She had been mostly free of it during her time at Wally Ochse's scummy abode but had begun to feel it creeping back in the closer she got to home. She supposed it was possible reading and handling Lucy's diary had enhanced the spirit's hold on her. She also thought it likely something larger than a mere haunting was at work here.

Bottom line though—she didn't much care.

Maybe her desires originated in some way from the dead woman, but knowing this made them no less intense or thrilling. She felt delightfully wicked. Debauched. It was nice to really let go, to shrug off the constraints of modern society and embrace something more primal. This was also evident in the way she savored the feel of the gritty earth beneath her bare feet. She felt one with nature, but not in that sensitive, hippy-dippy, tree-hugging way. The truth about nature was that it was raw, wild, and violent, and so was she now.

"Stop right here."

The bum's shoulders sagged as he came to a reluctant stop and turned around to look at her. He fingered his dog tags again and regarded her with eyes that looked clearer and saner than before. "You're one of them, ain't ya?"

Okay, scratch the "saner" part of that equation.

Arrianne smiled and arched an eyebrow. "Oh? Do you think so?"

He nodded and made a weird snuffling sound deep in his throat. "You're one of them shadow devils. A devil wearing a temptress mask."

The report of the gun made Arrianne's ears ring.

The bum's right knee exploded where she shot it. The bright bloom of red alone was nearly enough to bring Arrianne to the brink of orgasm. It was so beautiful. So right. Destruction of flesh was an intoxicant without rival. Ben—or whatever his name was; she was becoming confused on that point—pitched over, landing on his back as he clutched his ruined knee with shaking hands. Tears spilled from his eyes as he howled his agony, a sound so large it seemed to fill the entire forest.

Arrianne approached him in an unhurried way, doing a slinky hip sway that was a product of extreme arousal. It was how she often felt after drinking too much wine and making out with her man as they danced to slow, sexy music. She felt like dancing now. So she did, the screams and pitiful, wailing whimpers of the man she had shot functioning as music.

Then she stopped dancing and stood over him.

He held up trembling hands, shaking his head in a weak,

pitiful way as tears continued to stream from his bleary eyes. "I'm sorry. So sorry."

"Too bad."

Arrianne shot him again, this time through the chest.

He was dead a few moments later. After she watched the light fade from his eyes, Arrianne returned the gun to her purse and tossed the purse aside. She then wriggled out of her capris and panties again and positioned herself so she was standing over the dead man's face. Her feet were planted to either side of his head. She stared down at him for a long moment, enjoying the juxtaposition of her dainty, toenail-painted feminine feet next to the dead bum's crusty, disgusting face. There was an essential wrongness to it that added to her arousal, which was already at a level that had her pussy dripping wet. Her body quivered with intense erotic need as she bit her bottom lip and lowered herself to him.

She let out a loud, ecstatic groan as she pressed her pussy to his mouth and began to grind against him. She pitched forward and braced her palms against the earth, her moans steadily growing higher pitched and quavering as she increased the tempo of her pelvic gyrations. An odd thing happened as she did this. She could swear she felt the dead man's tongue come alive and flick at her clit. At first she took this as a product of an overly stimulated imagination, but then the tongue slid up inside her. Her face contorted as she dug her fingers into the ground. She should have felt terrified at this development, but she did not. It only stoked her arousal further into the stratosphere. She continued thrusting her sex against the dead man's face while the ghost tongue sent her into orgasmic oblivion. After several minutes of this, she let out a scream so explosively loud it could have shattered cathedral windows.

Her tempo slowed considerably, and she soon raised up a little to look at the dead man's now very moist face. He was still as dead as he had been minutes earlier. Arrianne figured she should maybe get up now and put on her clothes, perhaps think about putting some distance between herself and the scene of the crime while she still could. But some other nameless, initially formless impulse kept her where she was a bit longer as she continued to admire the grimy, gross, ugly—yet somehow beautiful—visage of the first man she'd ever killed.

Then she smiled.

Lowered herself to him again.

And pissed all over him.

She tossed her head back and laughed with unrestrained abandon as the glorious perversity of it all filled her with an exultation unmatched by any other experience in her life. This was subsequently forgotten, however, as an abrupt tide of nausea sent her rolling away from the defiled corpse. She got shakily to her feet and staggered over to a big tree, where she held on to a low-hanging branch and retched uncontrollably for many seemingly endless minutes. It went on and on and on, and her effluvium contained slimy chunks of things she recognized from previous episodes—pieces of animals, etc.— but now she saw what she recognized as human eyeballs and genitalia.

When the retching at last ended, the delirium gripping her abated and was replaced with a total, all-consuming horror at what she had done. She cried and cried and muttered many helpless, hopeless, useless denials.

Then, some twenty minutes after entering the woods with the doomed old veteran, she at last pulled herself together, got dressed, and wobbled out of the woods. The dogs were overjoyed at her return. She tried to take some meager comfort in their happiness but was unable to do so as she put the car in gear and tried to find her way home. She thought about stopping when she spied the dead man's grimy old duffel still on the passenger-side floor. Logic dictated getting rid of it. It was evidence, a clear link between her and the heinous crime she'd committed. She frowned as she stared at its lumpy shape and wondered what might be inside.

The thought piqued her curiosity in a way that overrode her common sense. She decided she would take it home and get it into the house, maybe squirrel it away someplace where Chuck wouldn't be apt to discover it. That way she could take it out sometime for a leisurely examination of its contents. In light of what she'd done, it was a ghoulish thing to contemplate, a form of postmortem gloating. But she just couldn't help it. She wanted—no, *needed*—to see what was inside the bag.

She could always get rid of it later, right?

Right.

Rationalization firmly in place, Arrianne continued home.

CHAPTER FOURTEEN
BRYAN SMITH

It had started as one of those notions she would sometimes pursue out of a combination of boredom and her ceaseless desire to see what kind of random crazy shit she could get away with. Not for one moment prior had she really believed she could spring the infamous Nicci Forrestal from the asylum.

But Lily Fontana had done just that.

And it had been *easy.*

As the three of them—Lily, Nicci, and Eric—walked out of the facility and out to the visitors' parking lot earlier that afternoon, she kept expecting someone to come rushing out to reclaim the frail, wounded-looking asylum inmate. Surely, she thought, someone somewhere along the chain of command would note that no one by her name was authorized to sign Nicci out for the day, ostensibly to visit a terminally ill relation in a nearby hospital. But miraculously, that had not happened. The initial wild exhilaration of getting away with something so big was fading, however, as Lily was quickly learning that having a genuinely crazy person for a traveling companion was overrated.

Who knew, right?

"It wouldn't stop vomiting into my mouth."

Lily nodded. "Uh-huh. Right."

"It had this weird hand. Big, like a giant's hand, but all warty and knobby. It went all the way up inside me. It turned me on."

Lily pressed her lips together and glanced at the rear-view mirror. She had no idea what to say to that. "Hmm."

"It was a monster."

"Of course it was."

Lily suspected getting Nicci out would have been harder—if not impossible—during an earlier phase of her involuntary confinement. However, the institutional review board had recently declared her no longer a threat to anyone, despite an ongoing disconnect from reality. The review board subsequently authorized a transfer from the locked dormitory unit to a facility with a far more lax attitude when it came to security.

Even so, getting away with it had been very exciting indeed.

Now … not so much.

"There were pieces of Sam everywhere. I didn't kill him. I slipped on his cock and fell on my ass. It was like something out of The Three fucking Stooges, only with more cock. And more blood. Talbot had a monster cock. The mafia killed him. I ain't killed nobody and anybody says different don't know shit. Fuck you if you think I'm lying."

Lily smiled at Nicci's reflection. "Relax, sweetie. I believe you."

I also believe you'd benefit immensely from a frontal lobotomy.

Listening to the loon's random brain-salad mumbo jumbo had become tiresome, but it still beat the hell out of anything else she might feasibly be doing today. At least it was something different and weird, which were qualities she valued. Regular life was such a drag so much of the time. With the sole exception of Eric, the people inhabiting her little corner of the world were all unimaginative slugs and dullards. In her bleaker moments, she wondered whether the whole world might be that way. It was a depressing thing to imagine. A whole planet populated by simpletons. People like her double-digit-IQ uncle, for instance, a man who—despite his own deep intelligence deficit—couldn't stop yammering away about "sheeple" and conspiracy theories so absurd that being repeatedly struck in the head with a hammer was a prerequisite for believing in them.

Enforced daily proximity to such overwhelming stupidity might well have driven Lily to the brink of suicide had she not hit upon a brilliant coping mechanism. She possessed an active and vibrant imagination and desired a means of exercising it that involved something other than staring at a computer screen all day. Though she enjoyed creating the fantasy worlds of the stories she wrote, she needed something that got her out of the house. So she decided to engage the world around her in creative exercises that were part elaborate deception and part performance art.

With the aid of Eric, her frequent partner-in-crime, she thus embarked on a series of outrageously inappropriate endeavors and adventures. Things like crashing a funeral and pretending to be the grief-stricken young mistress of the deceased. Or like the time Eric helped her convince a local priest she was possessed by Satan. Or like ...

Well, you get the picture.

Early on, Lily had worried that maybe this time they were getting in a little over their heads. There was a world of difference between the type of obnoxious but ultimately harmless pranks they normally pulled and something like this. Here they were a little more solidly into an area one could accurately describe as not quite within the bounds of the strictly legal. They could get into some actual, serious trouble if their false pretenses were uncovered or if they failed to return Nicci to the facility within the next few hours.

But Lily had no intention of allowing either disastrous scenario to come to pass. She meant to have Nicci back at the asylum well before sundown. The whole point of the excursion had been to break into the house at Sixty-Five Stirrup Iron Road to see what effect a return to the scene of the crime would have on her. Which, okay, was maybe a little cruel, but it was looking like it wouldn't matter anyway because apparently the house was no longer uninhabited.

She parked her Ford Tempo at the side of the road near the long driveway that led up to the house. A glance in the direction of the house brought a flood of relief as she saw Eric returning from his information-seeking expedition at the front door.

He opened the door across from her and dropped into the front passenger seat. "That dude's an asshole."

"Who?"

138

Eric tilted his chin toward the house. "Guy who lives there. Motherfucker looks like Mitt Romney."

"Gross."

Eric laughed.

Lily frowned. "And you're sure he really lives there? He's not just some real estate agent checking the place out?"

Eric shook his head. "Nah. Got a glimpse inside. There's furniture and stuff. Definitely got the look of a currently inhabited abode."

"Shit."

"Yeah."

"So what now?" Lily looked at the house again. Despite her concerns regarding the risk they were taking, this development was a bitter disappointment. Today's scheme had started out looking as if it had the potential to become her greatest triumph yet in the field of "LARPURPing" (Live Action Role-Playing with Unsuspecting Retards and Pinheads), as she called it. Now it seemed the whole thing would end with a fizzle rather than the expected bang, which was a damned shame.

Lily sighed. "I guess we take her back to the loony bin."

"I'm no loony," Nicci quipped from the backseat. "I saw what I saw and it's not my fault nobody believes me."

Eric snorted. "You keep telling yourself that." He twisted in his seat and leered at her through the gap between the seats. "We read all about you on the Internet. Here's a newsflash, you goddamn lunatic. There's no such thing as monsters."

Nicci sneered. "That's what everybody thinks … until they come face to face with one. I'll suck your dick if you don't take me back to the nuthouse."

Eric cackled at the non-sequitur and winked at Lily, who rolled her eyes. "*Now* who's being insensitive to the plight of the mentally fucked in the head? Nuthouse. Jesus." He laughed again and shook his head. "Would you really suck my dick?"

"I would. And I'm really fucking good at it. I used to be a blowjob whore before I got sent away."

"How many dicks have you sucked in your life?"

She shrugged her bony shoulders and tugged at a strand

of her stringy hair. Dunno. Hundreds? Thousands? Hard to say for sure. But I'm sort of out of practice, what with being locked up the last ten years."

Eric nodded. "You could probably use a refresher course." He glanced at Lily. "You mind if I let this crazy chick gobble my knob?"

Lily glared at him. "Don't be stupid. Pretty sure the law frowns on taking advantage of bitches with diminished mental capacity."

"I am not a bitch. You got no right to judge me."

There was a fierce edge to Nicci's voice, a barely restrained rage that served as a disturbing reminder of her instability. Hearing it added fuel to Lily's growing belief that her grand scheme had been ill-conceived from the start. Based on what she knew of Nicci's case, she doubted she'd had anything to do with her brother's death. On the other hand, the state had spent the better part of a decade doping her to the gills. There was no telling how much additional damage had been done to her already-fractured psyche. The sooner they got this whack job back to the asylum, the better. Lily could then set about devising some bigger and better scheme, one preferably not involving mental patients and perhaps a little less flagrant disregard for the law.

Lily tried a placating tone. "You're right. I was out of line. I shouldn't have called you a bitch."

Nicci grunted. "Damn right. And besides, you're not my cousin, you fucking liar. You're the bitch, not me."

Lily nodded as she gave the key in the Tempo's ignition a twist, bringing the engine sputtering to life. "Again, you are absolutely correct. I lied about being your cousin to spring you from the asylum. That was wrong of me. I am a lying bitch. I will now atone for my sins by taking you back to where you belong. And then—"

Nicci let out a screech and flopped over in the backseat. Her body spasmed and her hands clawed at the upholstery. Lily, in a panic, popped her seatbelt loose and twisted around to get a better look at what was happening. Nicci's eyes had rolled back, and foam rushed from the corners of her mouth.

Her foot kicked against the rear window hard enough to crack the glass.

Lily looked at Eric. "Holy shit. The fuck is happening?"

Eric had gone pale and looked more rattled than she had ever seen him. "She's having some kind of fit. Ah, shit, what if she dies on us?"

Lily slugged him on the shoulder. Hard. "Don't say that."

Eric grimaced and gingerly put a hand to his shoulder. "Ouch."

Lily slugged him again.

Eric glared at her. "Goddammit! Stop doing that!"

Lily's heart was pounding so fast it felt like it would blast itself out of her chest at any second. Any remaining sense of fun or play utterly deserted her in those moments. She was suddenly embroiled in a situation that was a little too real for her taste, and it had happened so rapidly it made her head spin. "Do something, goddammit!"

Eric laughed. "What the fuck am *I* supposed to do? I've got no experience with this kind of shit."

The force of the spasms gripping Nicci's body abruptly began to diminish. Her muscles relaxed, and she began to breathe audibly through her mouth again. But any relief Lily felt at this development was short-lived thanks to the even odder thing that started happening next.

Nicci moaned in an unmistakably sexual way. She arched her back and hiked her skirt up over her waist, exposing bare thighs covered in a sheen of sweat. She slithered out of her panties and tossed them aside. The undergarment struck a flabbergasted Eric in the face before dropping to the floor. Nicci reached between her legs and slid the fingers of her right hand into her pussy. Her fingers flexed as she simultaneously rubbed her clit with the fingertips of her left hand. She moaned some more and whipped her head from side to side, flinging her stringy hair about in an increasingly wild orgasmic frenzy. The volume of her moans rose and steadily grew shriller, achieving a pitch that made the car's other occupants cringe.

Eric shook his head in wide-eyed, astonished wonder. "The fuck is this fucking psycho bitch doing?"

Lily gave him a look of squinty-eyed disbelief. "She's masturbating, you idiot."

Eric scowled right back at her. "I *know* that. But this has got to be the first ever documented case of anyone rubbing one out right after having a motherfucking seizure in the backseat of a stranger's car. I mean … goddamn."

"First of all, nothing about this will be documented in any way if I can help it." Lily grimaced as Nicci lifted her ass off the seat and began to thrust her pelvis at an imaginary lover's groin. Her hands had come away from her pussy to clutch again at the upholstery. She let out a nasty, chuffing, spittle-spewing grunt with each thrust of her pelvis.

"Secondly, sit the fuck down and strap in because I'm about to burn rubber back to the goddamn asylum, where we are gonna dump this crazy bitch out and then hopefully never fucking see her again."

And Lily had every intention of doing just that.

Except something even more insane happened in the very next instant.

Nicci began to *levitate*.

Eric reeled backward, his back cracking against the dash behind him. "Holy mother of fuck!"

Lily was inclined to agree with that sentiment. There could be no doubt regarding the reality of what she was seeing. It was no carefully or cannily crafted illusion enhanced by gravity-defying gymnastics, a feat Nicci wouldn't have been capable of performing anyway. This was a genuine case of something unnatural—or supernatural—occurring in the backseat of Lily's fucking Ford Tempo, a notion that would have seemed hilarious were it not so goddamn terrifying. She was floating in midair, with her head tilted back and her hair hanging down. Her mouth was open wide and was continuing to emit those high-pitched squeals of ecstasy.

Nicci's legs were open wide and positioned in a way that made them look as if they were hooked over the shoulders of some invisible lover. There were finger-sized dimples in the flesh around her shoulders. The invisible whatever-it-was was holding her in place above the seat while it was apparently fucking the living shit out of her.

Lily realized the car was bouncing on its springs.

Nicci opened her mouth even wider and screamed as her feet shot upward and kicked at the roof of the car.

Eric groaned. "Fuuuuuuuuuuuck this."

Lily nodded. "Abandon ship."

They bailed and took several staggering backward steps away from the car, unable to avert their eyes from the otherworldly manifestation even as they sought distance from it. Lily's heart was doing that manic jackhammer thing in her chest again. Along with her fear came a number of paradigm-shifting realizations, beginning with the newly discerned knowledge that, holy shit, ghosts are real. This fact alone implied several other mind-shattering things. For instance, if ghosts existed, so could a host of other supernatural phenomena, including monsters. Nicci claimed she had been assaulted by a monster on this very property, the same monster that had torn her brother into a million itty bitty pieces. The preponderance of evidence therefore now suggested that Nicci had been telling the truth all along.

Which meant—

Lily turned her back on the car and started moving down the road at a rapid clip.

Eric called out after her. "Hey! Where are you going?"

"Away."

"Away where?"

She shrugged. "Just away." She glanced over her shoulder and saw that Eric hadn't moved. He remained captivated by what was happening in the car. The expression on his face conveyed equal measures of awe and dismay. "Are you coming or not?"

The car stopped bouncing before he could answer.

Lily stopped in her tracks. She was a good twenty yards or more down the road by the time one of the Tempo's rear doors popped open and a wobbly, loose-limbed Nicci emerged, looking like a drunk leaving a bar after last call.

Eric's look of dismay gave way to an expression of intense concern as he immediately went to her aid.

Lily wanted to scream at him, "No! Stay back!" but said nothing.

Eric glanced her way. "She needs help." He shifted his attention back to Nicci, who looked dazed and unable to focus. "Are you okay? Do you need—"

Nicci pitched toward him, her mouth opening wide as she vomited all over his chest. It was an explosion of slime-coated, unidentifiable chunks of organic objects, undigested meat of some kind. There was so much of it Lily knew there was no way Nicci's stomach could have held it all.

No *natural* way.

Eric shoved her away and started moving in Lily's direction.

But something stopped him.

Lily whimpered. "No. Please, no."

The same invisible something that had fucked Nicci in the back of the Tempo had seized Eric and was easily holding him in place. At least Lily assumed it was the same creature. She would hate to think there was more than one of the goddamn things.

The unseen thing had hold of Eric by the head. This was evidenced in the way he was able to freely move the rest of his body. He thrashed wildly and tried to kick at the thing holding him, but it was too strong.

While he struggled, Nicci started up the driveway toward the house. She still looked like a drunk, weaving and wobbling precariously from side to side as she walked.

Lily desperately wanted to help Eric. He was the only person in the whole world who really understood her and didn't judge her for being weird. A voice in her head screamed at her to go to him, but a deeper, more primal instinct recognized this for the suicidal foolishness it was and kept her rooted to the spot.

Eric stopped struggling and began to scream.

The reason why became immediately apparent.

The thing holding him was compressing the sides of his head. Eric's tongue protruded from his mouth, and blood leaked from the corners of his eyes. Then came a crunching sound as the shape of his head began to change.

Lily's stomach churned as she realized it was the sound of his skull being crushed.

The end came maybe a full second later.

Eric's head burst in an explosion of red.

Lily screamed.

Then she took off running as fast as she could.

CHAPTER FIFTEEN
BRYAN SMITH
AND BRIAN KEENE

The line went dead, and Chuck stared at the phone clutched in his trembling hand. The rapid *thump-thump-thump* of his heart underlined a growing sense of losing control. As a man who had long-prided himself on always having his shit together in all areas of his life, this descent into a state of deep doubt and disarray was especially tough to take. What made it even worse was the dizzying rapidity of the unraveling, which effectively negated his usual ability to take command of a situation and put things right in an efficient and methodical way.

A spasm shot through his stomach and bowels. He belched, grimacing at the taste of acid. He suddenly felt lightheaded. As another cramp tore through him, Chuck sank to the floor. His strength seemed to bleed from him. Nauseated and faint, he drew his knees up to his chest, lowered his head between them, and focused on taking slow, deep breaths. He sat there a full ten minutes before the panic ebbed, and when it did, he carefully got to his feet again.

The rain of shit pouring down on him simply had to cease at some point soon or he might well become as seemingly unhinged as the women in his life. Obviously some nefarious dark force was conspiring against him. A lunatic notion perhaps, but how else to explain what was happening? Because somehow it wasn't enough that his more-or-less sweet and beloved wife had decided it would be fun to wallow in a level of depravity so epically perverse and disgusting it would make de Sade himself blow chunks. Oh, no. Things clearly needed to be a lot more interesting than that. Hence the revelation that his gorgeous former mistress was now his current gorgeous psycho stalker.

Flavia had made it clear she was not even close to being done with him. Moreover, she would *never* be done with him, not as long as they both drew breath. Which was maybe a bit of an exaggeration since spurned women have been lashing out at the men who dumped them since the dawn of time.

But there were always exceptions. The ones who couldn't let go of their anger and allowed it to morph into obsession. Sometimes they made the news, for things like setting the homes of their former lovers on fire or for stabbing them a truly excessive amount of times. Chuck shuddered. The whole *Fatal Attraction* trip: he could totally imagine Flavia boiling his proverbial pet rabbit in a stew, just like in that old movie.

I'm closer than you think. Those had been her last words before clicking off the line. The implication was obvious—she was threatening him. Maybe it wasn't a promise to do physical violence—though that was a possibility he unfortunately could not dismiss—but he did believe it meant she would attempt to complicate his life in some way. The most likely scenario involved her coming to his house to cause a scene. And she would probably want to do it when she could be certain Arrianne would be home to bear witness to his shame.

Hell, she could be lurking somewhere down the street right now, just waiting for his wife to pull into the drive. If so, all hell could be about to break loose. It could be the beginning of the end of everything. That was maybe an overdramatic generalization, but it would certainly spell the end of this phase of his life.

Next step: divorce court.

Chuck put his face in his hands and made a sound somewhere between a moan and a despairing laugh. He honestly wasn't sure whether he should be depressed over that possibility or relieved. Maybe divorce and relocation to another fucking state was the only way he might be able to get his life back on an even keel. Later he could settle down with a normal, more stable woman—if such a creature existed.

His stomach cramped again. Hoping to stave off another panic attack, he went back into the kitchen and grabbed the whiskey off the shelf, this time taking a healthy slug straight from the bottle. After taking a second slug, he leaned against the counter and let out a big breath.

Calm down, he thought. *You can get through this, one way or another. You've just got to calm—*

A big *BOOM!* from somewhere else in the house made him jump. He also screamed like a little girl, but this was a detail he knew he would never share with anyone. The sound came again, and he walked out of the kitchen to stand at the foot of the staircase to the second floor.

The sound came yet again.

Yep. Definitely up there.

It sounded like someone repeatedly slamming a heavy door. But that made no sense. No one else was in the house. Right?

He put a hand on the banister.

Ascended the first two steps.

BOOM!

And then one more.

BOOM!

At that point he was able to ascertain two things. One, he was reasonably certain the sound was coming from the attic. Two, he was apparently suffering from temporary insanity. Nothing else could explain his apparent intent to investigate the scary noise.

He told himself he was being ridiculous. What he was hearing was probably related to their earlier problems with pests.

He nodded.

Right. Really, really *big chipmunks.*

That's what's up there.

He moved up another step.

Then he jumped and shrieked again at another loud sound. He stumbled and spent a moment clinging to the banister for balance as he whimpered like a baby. Yet another detail he would leave out of the narrative in the unlikely event he ever shared the story of this day with anyone else.

The new sound came again.

He realized it was someone banging on the front door.

He stood very still for a moment, waiting to hear the sound from the attic again, but the source of it had mysteriously fallen silent. However, the person on the other side of the front door was still pounding away at it. He made a sound of self-pitying disgust as he stood there and nervously ran a hand through his hair. It was possible the person on the porch could be Arrianne. She could be struggling with the dogs and maybe some packages. That was plausible.

But in his gut he knew it was Flavia. It had to be.

In which case, he had better deal with her now. It would be unpleasant as fuck, but maybe—just maybe—he could somehow convince her to go on her merry way before Arrianne returned, thus miraculously averting total disaster.

Which didn't seem likely, but whatever. He'd find a way to deal with it.

The pounding continued—insistent, heavy ... almost frantic.

He descended the stairs and went to the front door, where he stood for another long moment, hesitating again as he watched the door rattle in its frame. This wasn't just a case of someone trying to get his attention—it was an indicator of deep agitation.

The hammering blows continued. Beneath them, he thought he heard a woman sobbing.

Some of Chuck's apprehension began to give way to anger. *I have seriously fucking had it with this crazy bitch.*

He unlocked the door and flung it open, expecting to confront Flavia. Instead, what he found left him momentarily stunned.

A young woman stood on the porch, both fists raised in an apparent effort to continue her assault on the door. She was probably in her early twenties, Chuck surmised, and attractive in a not-really-trying-to-be-and-couldn't-really-give-a-fuck sort of way. Her ears, nose, and bottom lip were pierced. She wore no makeup, but her high cheekbones and baby-blue eyes stood out anyway. Her long blonde hair and straight bangs were pretty, if somewhat disheveled, and currently plastered to her forehead with sweat. Her face was panic-stricken, and she'd obviously been crying, but when she saw Chuck, her expression of relief was almost comical.

149

Before he could speak, she tumbled into the foyer and darted past him.

"Hey!" Leaving the door hanging open, Chuck spun around. "Excuse me ... can I help you?"

"Shut the door," she begged. "Please, mister. You've got to help me. Eric ... she ..."

"Slow down. Who are you, and what the hell is going on?"

"She ... and then ... oh, God, she's coming. She's after me. Shut the fucking door!"

Chuck stood there gaping, one hand on the door, trying to process what was happening. A young woman—obviously distraught and most likely having just experienced some sort of altercation or accident—barged into his home and was babbling about someone named Eric and an unspecified woman who might be the cause of the distress.

Could it be Flavia? Could she have been lurking outside the house, and for some reason have attacked this girl? And who was Eric? Hadn't that been the name of the kid who had shown up earlier, asking if there were any odd jobs available?

"Please," the girl sobbed. "Please, mister. I can explain everything. But please, just shut the fucking door before she finds us!"

"Before who finds us?" Chuck asked.

"Nicci fucking Forrestal!"

"Who?" Chuck frowned. The name struck a subtle, familiar chord, but he didn't know why.

"Goddamn it!" The girl grabbed his shoulders. Her nails dug through his shirt and into his skin. "Please, please, please help me. We've got to call the cops or something. She ... it killed Eric! He was—" The rest was lost in unintelligible sobs.

Chuck gently but firmly grabbed her wrists and pulled her nails from his skin. Then he led her toward the kitchen. "Come on," he said. "It'll be okay. Just try to calm down, okay? I can't help you unless I understand what's going on."

If the girl heard him or understood, she gave no indication. But she did allow him to guide her to the kitchen table. She sat down, balled her fists in her lap, and stared at the floor. Her shoulders shook as she cried.

Chuck opened the fridge and got her a bottle of water. He unscrewed the cap and set it down in front of her. After a moment's thought, he grabbed a tissue box from the counter and set it on the table as well.

The girl wiped her eyes and blew her nose, balling up the tissues and placing them in her lap when she was done. She ignored the water but raised her head to meet Chuck's inquisitive stare.

"Let's start over," he said. "What's your name?"

"L-lily. Lily ... Fontana."

"Okay. Good. Now, what's happened, Lily? Were you in an accident?"

"We ... Eric and I ... we thought it might be fun to spring Nicci from the loony bin. Sort of a day trip, you know? I said we should ... we should bring her back here to the scene of the ... where everything happened ... and we'd film it maybe ... and ..."

Chuck gestured at her to pause. "To the scene of what, Lily? I'm not following you. Who are Nicci and Eric? And what's this about a loony bin?"

Lily took a deep, shuddering breath and then sipped some water. When she started talking again, she seemed to regain her composure. "Eric is ... was ... my friend. Not really a boyfriend, although we've fucked around a few times. He was fun, I guess. Is it me, or is it hot in here?"

As Chuck watched, Lily tugged at her clothing. She seemed to study his reaction. Perplexed, he cleared his throat.

Then she continued. "Eric wasn't really one to take the lead. Sort of vanilla. But he was open to trying new things. Know what I mean?"

"Look," Chuck said, "I wasn't asking about your sex life. You barged into my home, acting like someone had been murdered. You're not being very rational right now. I think either you should explain what's going on or leave before I call the police."

"Call the police," Lily urged. "Definitely. I'm sorry ... it's just ... I don't know what I was thinking. Maybe I'm just in shock. For a minute, I didn't feel like myself."

"That's okay. Perfectly understandable, given the circumstances. So what happened to Eric?"

Lily's expression darkened. "He ... something killed him. His head ..."

"Was it this Nicci you mentioned?"

"No. I mean, it happened at the same time she got ... taken over. Fucked by a ghost. Whatever you want to call it. But I don't think it was her."

Chuck decided to ignore the odd statement. Obviously the girl was not thinking clearly or behaving rationally. He tried to direct the conversation with more pointed questions, hoping to divine the facts.

"When you first came in, you said she was after you."

"Did I?" Lily pulled at her clothing again, flashing more skin. "Well, I was pretty shook up. But no, she didn't kill Eric. Don't get me wrong. Nicci is absolutely batshit fucking crazy, but something else killed Eric. I think she's connected to it, in some way."

"Connected to what? Your friend's murder?"

"No. Whatever the fuck it was that happened here in your house. I don't think she did it. I mean, I thought so until tonight, but after what I just saw? No fucking way."

"What are you talking about?"

"You know, the death of her brother and all that?"

Chuck stared at her for a moment. His breath caught in his throat. He blinked twice. "Oh my God," he said. "Nicci Forrestal. Her brother was Sam Forrestal. He used to own this house. I *knew* I recognized that name! That's who you're talking about?"

Lily nodded.

"And she's here? She's outside my house?"

"Yeah. She left the car before I did. She was heading this way. But I lost sight of her as I ran."

Chuck shook his head, even more confused than before. But before he could continue with his questions, the noises in the attic resumed with a renewed frenzy. They were loud enough that Lily jumped in her chair.

"Chipmunks," Chuck said, nodding toward the ceiling.

"At least I think they're chipmunks."

"Chipmunks? Sounds more like a fucking rhinoceros, mister ...?"

"Chuck. My name is Chuck. And you're right. It's getting louder. That's too loud to be chipmunks."

They both fell quiet for a moment, listening as the cacophony increased. It sounded to Chuck as if someone was dragging something heavy across the attic floor. The sound unnerved him but was also deceptively lulling. Focused on the noises from upstairs, Chuck realized that for a minute, he'd forgotten all about the threat of Flavia or the possible appearance of a crazy woman who had killed her brother, in addition to Lily's friend, in this very home.

Chuck had more questions for Lily—like why Eric had visited the house earlier, how Nicci had escaped from custody, and what exactly they had hoped to achieve—but as the pounding in the attic grew louder, panic set in again. It would have been bad enough if Arrianne had returned home to find Flavia here, but with all these new wrinkles and drama? There would be no way he could explain it to her. Hell, he didn't understand it himself.

The thought came again that Flavia could be the cause of the noises. Then an even more frightening idea: What if it wasn't Flavia? What if Nicci Forrestal had broken into the house and was upstairs? After all, the noises had immediately preceded Lily's arrival. What if Nicci had gotten here before her? Or what if the two were working together, along with that Eric kid? Maybe this had all been some kind of scam just to gain access to the house.

He realized Lily was breathing heavily. Her eyes seemed glazed and unfocused. The tip of her very pink tongue licked her parted lips. Beneath the thin fabric of her damp shirt, her nipples stood out like rivets. "I feel ... funny," she said. "Don't know what's ..."

As she trailed off, Chuck reached for his cell phone, intent on calling the police. Lily didn't seem to notice. When he thumbed the phone's screen, however, he was shocked to find a porn video playing. He cringed in disgust. On the screen, two women were lathing a man's cock with their tongues, but that wasn't what had repulsed him. It was the obscene number of large, knobby genital warts covering the man's cock—and how the women paid special, loving attention to each of them, administering oral favors to each misshapen wart in turn. They flicked the tips of their tongues across each bump and then sucked on the warts.

He quickly glanced up to see if Lily had caught sight of the perverse spectacle, but her attention seemed focused elsewhere. Thankful that he'd kept the phone muted, Chuck tried to exit the video and place his emergency call—only to discover that the phone was seemingly locked. No matter what he did, he couldn't get the video to stop. None of the phone's other features would work. He then noticed that the device was growing hot in his hand. "Fucking piece of shit ..."

Frustrated, he placed the phone face down on the table and stood up.

Lily slowly shook her head, as if waking from a dream, and stared at him in puzzlement. "Where are you going?"

"I think we should call the police."

She nodded. Chuck noticed that she was rubbing the inside of her thigh with one hand. He couldn't tell if she was even aware of it.

"There's something wrong with my cell phone," he told her. "Hang on a second."

He reached for the house phone and took it off its cradle, but when he brought it to his ear, there was no dial tone. Chuck tried it several times but was rewarded with more silence. Just as he was about to hang up, he heard something on the other end of the line—the distinct sound of a woman in the throes of orgasm.

"Hello?" he said into the receiver. "Is someone there?"

The feminine moans of ecstasy were replaced by a succession of different sounds—the crack of a whip, the smack of flesh striking flesh, a dog barking, a man grunting, what might have been a goat, some type of machine starting up, and finally, someone vomiting. Frustrated and disgusted, Chuck hung up.

"The phone isn't working," he said. "Do you have a cell phone, Lily?"

She shook her head. "It's in my car. And I don't want to go back there. Eric ... he ... his head was—"

BOOM!

The kitchen lights shook, swaying back and forth, as what sounded like a bowling ball being dropped echoed from the attic again and again.

"Fuck this," Chuck said. He opened a drawer next to the sink and pulled out the longest butcher knife he could find.

"Fuck me," Lily responded.

"It's okay," he said, trying to reassure her. "I just want to check out what's going on."

"No. I meant that I want you to fuck me. Right here, on the table. I want you to eat me. I'll put it on a plate for you, if you want. Just lick me. I need to feel your mouth on me."

"I-I ..." Chuck stammered. "You said your friend is dead. There's something in my attic. I don't think now is—"

"I know it doesn't make any sense," Lily interrupted. "It's fucking crazy. But I can't help it. Ever since I got here, I just feel ... I need you to lick me, Chuck. I need you to fuck me. Not want you to. *Need* you to. Please?"

Loathe as he was to admit it, a big part of Chuck was turned on at the prospect. He felt embarrassed by the realization, but it occurred to him that he'd been feeling that way a lot in regard to sexuality lately. It was almost as if moving to this house had awakened some hidden perversity within him. Except that was ridiculous. More likely, it was just stress and frustration. He needed a healthy outlet. That hadn't worked with Flavia, and he was fairly certain a dalliance with Lily would have the same outcome.

He opened his mouth to explain that he was married but then thought better of it. There was no telling what was wrong with this girl, and he still had no idea what was really going on. Instead, he decided to try to appease her. "I ... as tempting as that sounds, Lily, I won't be able to focus until I know what's going on upstairs. I'm going to go check it out."

"Okay." She smiled. "But I'm coming with you. I don't

want to sit here alone."

Chuck headed for the stairs, his attention divided between the noises from the attic and the girl creeping along behind him.

What Chuck and Lily didn't notice was that every computer and television in the house were now switched on, and all of them were showing the same video that had been on his cell phone.

CHAPTER SIXTEEN
BRIAN KEENE
AND JACK KETCHUM

Flavia crouched in the shadows beneath the tree line, just at the edge of the woods, a football field's distance from Chuck's house. She'd been there several hours, and her joints and muscles ached from remaining hidden for so long. It had been warm and sunny when she first arrived, but the woods had grown cold after the sun set, and she shivered, clad only in jeans and a thin, flimsy blouse. Worse than the cold were the insects—spiders and gnats and ticks, all seemingly vying for a chance to crawl on her, bite her, and otherwise make her scream. It was a testament to her dedication that she had not, in fact, shrieked or otherwise given away her location, especially when a particularly large and ugly spider had dropped from a tree limb directly into her cleavage. A testament to her dedication—and to how mad she was at Chuck right now.

In addition to being cold and miserable and angry, Flavia was also horny. She couldn't explain it, but ever since her arrival—from the moment she'd parked the car on the dirt road, hiding it from view, and then hiking through the woods to her current hiding spot—she'd been aroused. It was a state that had no ebb or peak. It just kept building and building. Despite the insects and her uncomfortable surroundings, she'd been tempted to masturbate several times. With each occurrence, it had been more difficult for her to fight the urge.

She'd just finished talking to Chuck, carefully shielding her cell phone's screen so the light wouldn't be seen from the house, when she noticed the car. It was parked along the side of the road, halfway between her location and Chuck's house. Flavia supposed it had been there all along. She certainly hadn't seen it pull up, and its engine wasn't idling. The only reason she noticed it now was because a young man was walking toward it. He seemed to be coming from the direction of Chuck's house, but Flavia couldn't be sure. From her vantage point, she could only see the side of the house and the backyard. The front door and driveway were hidden from view.

The car's dome light came on as the young man opened the passenger door and slid inside. Flavia was able to discern two other figures inside the vehicle. Then the kid shut the door and the light vanished.

All was quiet again, save for the insects and birds. Something rustled overhead, startling Flavia. She glanced up and saw that it was just a squirrel. The rodent cocked its head and stared at her. Flavia stared back.

Time passed. She debated what to do next.

Then the screams started.

They were muffled. Distant. At first, she couldn't determine their location. Then Flavia realized they were coming from inside the car. As she watched, the back door opened and a young woman stumbled out. She walked funny, as if she'd just done a gang bang with an entire basketball team. The woman shuffled toward Chuck's house.

What the hell?

"Hey," Flavia called, her voice quavering. "Over here! Are you hurt?"

If the woman heard her, she gave no indication. Instead, she hurried on. Flavia was about to call out again when she heard branches rustling behind her.

"Don't do that again," a voice said.

Gasping, Flavia turned. A man stood behind her, half-hidden in the shadows.

"Don't call out," he said. "Calling out would be stupid. First of all, you're a football field away from the action. You're gonna need a very loud voice. Maybe even a megaphone."

"W-who the fuck are you?"

Smiling, a handsome older man with beautiful dark hair and even darker, intoxicating eyes stepped out from behind the tree. He was dressed simply in a black T-shirt and jeans, and Flavia could see that he was in shape. She caught a whiff of cigarettes and scotch, but it was a pleasant, almost soothing aroma.

"I'm Jack Ketchum."

He was still smiling, but Flavia detected a hint of sadness in his expression.

"I ..." Flavia paused. She suddenly felt dizzy. "I ... what are you doing out here?"

He moved closer. "The thing is, Flavia, my buddies have painted me into a corner here. I'm in an untenable position. But it's up to me to fix it."

"What the hell are you talking about?"

"Let me explain. Arrianne is on her way home with the dogs after murdering a foul-smelling Vietnam vet whose name she can't remember. Nicci's headed up the driveway toward the house after getting bonked in midair. Lily's in the house trying to fuck Chuck after watching Eric's head explode, and they're about to investigate the chipmunks in the attic."

"Wait ... you know Chuck and Arrianne?"

"In a sense. But that's not important right now. And I'd really like to know where Keene ran off to. He was just here a little while ago, watching you with me."

"Who?"

"Never mind. He said something about the location of Lily's car. It was parked in the driveway. Then along the road. Which is it? Maybe he went to fix that."

"I don't know what you're talking about."

"Well, obviously we're moving toward the climax here. And to get there, we need to get everybody into the house, or else why would the damn thing be called Sixty-Five Stirrup Iron Road, right? But see, everybody includes you, Flavia."

"Listen, Jack—"

"No, you listen. You're hiding in the woods a hundred yards away when you see Nicci staggering toward the house. You call out to her. I have problems with that. It doesn't fly with me. Your reaching out to Nicci in any way imaginable goes totally against your previously established character. You're a selfish, single-minded little slut without a generous bone in your body."

"Fuck you! You don't know a thing about me."

"Actually, I do. I created you. And I've got major problems

with your actions here. Finally—and most importantly— if you saw Nicci stumbling fuck-drunk out of the car, didn't you also see Eric's head blown all to hell right afterward? And if so, would you run to the house after seeing that? Fuck no, you wouldn't. You'd get the hell out of there. You'd live to stalk another day."

Flavia realized Ketchum had gotten closer to her while he'd been talking, yet she hadn't been aware of him moving. She took a step backward, steeling herself to flee. "I don't know what your problem is, asshole, but I'm warning you. Don't fuck with me."

"My problem, as I see it, is you. And here's how I solve it. It's simple and elegant. I eliminate you. That's right. No, Flavia. You're not hiding in the woods. You're not calling out to Nicci. You're not here at all. *You don't exist.* In fact, you've *never* been here."

"You're fucking crazy. You so much as touch me and I'll—"

Flavia's threat faltered as Ketchum pulled a knife from his jeans. It was impossibly big—far too long and broad to have fit in his shallow jeans pocket, yet there it was.

"How did you—?"

"I can do anything I want. Anything at all. Now don't move."

"Fuck you." Flavia turned to run and found that she couldn't. Her feet remained firmly in place, legs locked at the knees.

"You can't do this," Flavia cried. "It's not fair!"

"Why not? Who the hell's writing this chapter, you or me? Look, Flavia. The story doesn't need you. You're excess baggage. There are already plenty of characters here. None of them very likeable and none of them terribly well-defined. So I'm suggesting to my friends that we just kill them off as quickly and gruesomely as possible and get it over with. Except for the dogs. We don't hurt the dogs. And hopefully, one of them will get Dickie's flea and tick thing taken care of at some point. That shit's annoying."

Sobbing, Flavia began to tremble. She willed herself to

move, but her legs ignored the commands.

Ketchum placed a hand on her shoulder, and she stared into his eyes. The darkness within them seemed bottomless.

"What the hell kind of name is Flavia, anyway? Who would name their kid *Flavia?* Or a character in their book for that matter? Maybe some pervert who's seen that twisted Italian rebel-nun movie too many times. But I mean, come on. *Flavia?* And why would you want to stalk an asshole like Chuck in the first place? Papa Bear is a first-rate asshole. Makes no sense. So you're a goner. You okay with that?"

Flavia moaned—a hopeless and mournful sound.

Ketchum thrust the knife under her left breast. "Good," he said. "I feel a whole lot better. Now let's get on with the story."

CHAPTER SEVENTEEN
JACK KETCHUM
AND J. F. GONZALEZ

Arrianne pulled the Tempo into the driveway. She wondered briefly who their visitors were and why they'd left the backseat passenger door wide open.

Delivery?

She hauled the duffel bag up from the passenger-side of the floor and opened up her own back door to let the dogs out.

Dickie was licking his balls. Assiduously. Little Lucy was helping him. She'd never seen a puppy do that before but figured what the hell. A dog's gotta do what a dog's gotta do, right?

And who was she to judge?

She figured they were bonding.

Arrianne paused, trying to remember when, exactly, Lucy had gotten out of her crate. It seemed like letting the puppy out was something she'd have remembered doing, yet she couldn't recall. Shrugging, she chalked it up to absentmindedness.

She clapped. "C'mon, Dickie! C'mon, Lucy."

The dogs just looked at her for a moment, as if to say, *So you've got a better party?* and then snuffed and harrumphed and lumbered off the car seat.

The duffel was heavy. She shouldered it manfully and deposited it on the floor of the garage. It clanked. Something metal inside.

Arrianne looked down at the duffel bag, debating whether she should take it inside the house. She'd have to open it eventually, especially if she intended to go through with her hastily conceived plan.

She cast a glance over at the dogs. They were sitting on the concrete floor, looking at her expectantly. "You guys stay right there," she said as she reached for the garage door opener. She pressed the button, and the garage door descended on its corrugated track.

She flipped on the light switch as the door ground to a close and paused for a moment. Lucy and Dickie remained sitting on their haunches, still gazing up at her.

For the first time in weeks she felt lucid, in control. She remembered everything vividly—remembered the torture she'd put Brad Zeller through, how she'd hurt him. She knew intellectually that she'd committed murder, that she'd done something that went against her very moral fiber, but she knew she hadn't *really* done it. It had been somebody else, some*thing* else, controlling her every move, pushing her buttons, *making* her do it.

It had infected her with its own essence, injecting its own carnal desires into her.

She realized this shortly after killing Brad/Ben. And while she was sorry for what had happened, she knew that she wasn't really at fault. It had been the spirit of Lucy Pearson who had possessed her.

And she had just the thing to send that nasty bitch back to the hell she'd come from.

She'd found it in the duffle bag Brad had been carrying. There were two of them, and she instantly recognized them.

Pressure cookers.

Brad Zeller had said something about staying one step ahead of those creatures. She knew what creatures he was talking about now. The Southeast Asian jungle had been rife with them. That much was apparent by his descriptions of the depravity he and his fellow GIs had committed on those hapless South Vietnamese villagers.

And it was obvious to her now that Brad had been intending to silence those creatures forever due to the presence of those pressure cookers. When she came across him, he'd been heading east toward the house. She still wasn't sure what the connection was between Lucy Pearson and the creatures he'd experienced in Vietnam. Maybe Lucy had become some kind of succubus or something. Maybe creatures like that were prevalent in Southeast Asia, and Brad had recognized the activity at Sixty-Five Stirrup Iron Road. After all, he'd said the creatures were after him. Maybe they'd somehow found him. Maybe Sixty-Five Stirrup Iron Road was some kind of breeding ground for them. She wasn't sure of Lucy Pearson's life prior to the events in the diary, but she had to wonder if Lucy had become infected shortly after moving to this house. And she wondered if, instead of becoming horrified, Lucy had embraced the depravity the creatures had introduced her to.

Arrianne regarded the duffel bag for a moment. The dogs remained seated, looking at her with their soulful eyes. Somebody was in the house with Chuck. She didn't know who, but her guess was Lucy had something to do with it. Lucy had somehow drawn them to the house.

Arrianne had to get Chuck out of here. But first she had to set this pressure cooker up out here in the garage.

"One in the garage, the other in the living room," she said as she bent down, unzipped the duffel bag, and brought out the first pressure cooker.

Then she set it up.

It never occurred to her that she shouldn't know how to do that.

The noise in the attic intensified as Chuck and Lily headed upstairs to the second floor.

BOOM!

Chuck paused briefly, heart pounding. *That can't be a bunch of chipmunks.*

Lily was trying to grab at him from behind. "C'mon, Chuck, forget about what's going on up there. You need to pay more attention to what's going on down *here!*" She moved his hand down to the crotch of her shorts and pressed it there.

Chuck pulled away roughly. "Either come with me, or get the fuck out of my house."

Lily huffed. "You don't have to be such an asshole about it."

Chuck ignored her and reached the second-floor hallway. He rounded the corner where the stairway to the attic was and paused for a moment.

What the fuck?

Chuck tensed and started up the stairs, determined to get to the bottom of this. Call it intuition, but he had a feeling

somebody was up there. Lily followed hot on his heels, and
then he was entering the attic. For a minute he was so stunned
by what he saw that he stopped.

Lily bumped into him. "You want to do it here? Sure, we
can do it here, stud. Turn around, and I'll get on my knees and
blow you right here."

There was another loud boom, and this time he saw the
cause of it.

A stocky guy with short, salt-and-pepper hair was sitting
on a large cardboard box, bouncing a large rubber ball on the
wooden floor. *BOOM! BOOM! BOOM!*

The guy looked over at them. "Finally! Took you long
enough to get your asses up here. Didn't you hear me?"

Chuck gaped. "Who the hell are you?"

"Why don't we wait for Arrianne to finish preparing the
second pressure cooker," the man said. "By then, maybe the
other guys will get here."

"Oh boy, more guys are coming," Lily said. "We can have
a gangbang!"

"Really?" The stranger eyed Lily as if she were incredibly
annoying, and then he shifted his attention to Chuck. "Your
wife's just exiting the garage with a pressure cooker. She's
just set one up in the garage. Call her up here. This concerns
both of you. We need to act quickly if we want to do this right
and finish on a high note."

"What the fuck are you talking about? And who are you?"
Chuck asked. He found that he wasn't angry yet. He wasn't
even scared. If anything, he was confused.

The stranger stood up. "Let's cut to the chase. I'm J. F.
Gonzalez. I didn't actually create you, but I helped breathe
some life into you. So did my friends, one of whom—Jack
Ketchum—has already taken care of Flavia."

"Jack Ketchup?" Lily asked.

At the mention of Flavia's name, Chuck felt a pit of dread.
"Flavia? What about her?"

Gonzalez clapped Chuck on the shoulder. "You don't need
to worry about her anymore, pal. She won't be stalking you
any longer." He winked at Chuck. "You horny rascal!" He

shouldered his way past Chuck and called down the stairs to the second and first floors. "Arrianne! Come on up here. We need to talk."

"What do you mean you didn't create me but you helped breathe life in to me?" Chuck asked. "I don't understand."

"It's like this, Chuck," Gonzalez said.

Chuck noticed he was dressed in black jeans, a black T-shirt, and a black leather jacket.

"You kinda turned into an asshole. I still have a little sympathy for Arrianne, but the rest of you I couldn't care less about. Don't get me wrong; things were moving nicely along, especially with the two bodies here in the attic. Throwaway characters, Zito and Jake. Those were all Keene's doing, but Keene never does anything without a reason. I'm guessing he meant to bring them back. Both of you would have been prime targets for their mayhem. Arrianne's already prone to Lucy's influence. But despite all that—"

"I don't understand," Chuck interrupted. "What the hell's going on?"

"That's the problem," Gonzalez said, shaking his head. "We don't know anymore. I'm all for a good gorefest every now and then, but some of the character motivations here are just ... it's just gone all sideways."

"Character motivations? What are you talking about?"

From downstairs, Arrianne called, "Chuck?"

Gonzalez called down. "We're up here! Come on up."

Arrianne sounded hesitant. "Chuck? Is someone up there with you?"

"It's okay, hon," Chuck said, keeping his gaze on Gonzalez.

Arrianne crept up to the attic. When she saw Gonzalez, her eyes widened. "Who are you?"

"Here's how we're going to play this." J. F. Gonzalez stepped forward. "I might not have created you two initially—that was Lee's doing. He set this whole thing in motion, and a bunch of us got in on the fun. And it *was* fun for a while. Most important, it's for a good cause. But like I said, the story's gone sideways, and it's not like we have an editor with us to redline the hell out of us, so we're going to have to fix things ourselves. Jack was right."

"Jack Ketchup?" Lily asked again.

Gonzalez corrected Lily. "Jack *Ketchum*." He reached into his jacket pocket. "Don't you fucking listen?"

Lily was fidgeting. Her eyes flicked from Gonzalez to Chuck and then to Arrianne. "I like girls too. We could do a four-way. Right here."

Gonzalez shook his head. "I'm married, sweetheart. But Harding, Southard, and Smith are single. And I imagine you wouldn't be their first four way, either. Now be still. Grownups are talking."

"They sound like fun," Lily insisted. "Invite them over."

"Jesus fucking Christ on a pogo stick, will you shut up?" Gonzalez looked like he was becoming more disgusted with Lily as time went on.

"I don't understand," Arrianne said. "What's going on?"

"You said this Jack Ketchum person already took care of Flavia," Chuck said. "Is she okay?"

"Flavia?" Arrianne asked. She looked at Chuck suspiciously. "Who's Flavia?"

"She can join in too!" Lily said, her smile wide and eager with the anticipation of sex.

Gonzalez pulled a black semiautomatic handgun out of his jacket pocket, pointed it at Lily's face, and pulled the trigger. Lily's head disintegrated in a spray of blood, bone, and brain matter, and she dropped like a slab of meat. The resounding boom caused Chuck and Arrianne to cry out and stagger back. Arrianne almost fell down the attic stairs.

"You—you just shot her!" Chuck exclaimed. His heart was pounding, fueled by the adrenaline running through his system.

"Yeah, I did." Gonzalez placed the handgun in his jacket and turned to Chuck. "She was getting on my fucking nerves."

"Please don't hurt us!" Arrianne said.

Gonzalez shook his head. "I don't think you have to worry about that. Did you set that second pressure cooker yet?"

"How did you—"

"It's a simple yes or no question, Arrianne."

"No."

"Good. Where are the dogs?"

"Downstairs in the kitchen."

Gonzalez nodded and cocked his head slightly, as if trying to listen.

Chuck's ears were still ringing from the gunshot, but he thought he could hear the dogs going bonkers downstairs, barking their heads off.

"They're fine," Gonzalez said. "Which is good. Ketchum would have our heads if anything happened to the dogs."

Chuck began to cry.

"Stop that," Gonzalez said. "Why don't we go downstairs and finish this?"

CHAPTER EIGHTEEN
J. F. GONZALEZ
AND NATE SOUTHARD

When they reached the kitchen, Gonzalez looked at the dogs and nodded. They immediately stopped barking and settled down. He turned to Chuck and Arrianne and motioned to the breakfast bar. "Have a seat. We should talk."

Chuck and Arrianne pulled up seats at the breakfast bar. Gonzalez sat opposite them. "Now, I would have preferred to have killed Lily as gruesomely as possible, but she was just too goddamn annoying. I'm hoping my friends have some ideas as to what to do with the rest of you, especially that Wally Ochse guy. God, he was a revolting character."

At the mention of the man who'd sold her Lucy Pearson's diary, Arrianne flinched. "Did you follow me? How did you know about him?"

"One of my friends created him. Did a great job with the whole backstory too. But we've got to get this over with and end the story as gruesomely as possible. By my count, this Ochse guy is the only scumbag left. Eric, Nicci, Flavia, and Lily are dead. It would be nice if we killed Wally off too. Then we'll have to make a decision about the two of you. Only thing I'm certain of is we're not going to hurt the dogs."

The front door opened and shut. A voice called out. "You sure? I wouldn't put it past Shane. Dude might do it just to mess with people."

A man entered. He was bald, with tired eyes and a beard flecked with gray and red. His jeans were a little too baggy for someone in his thirties, and he wore a green shirt that featured two cartoon kittens playing with a hand grenade. A sack of groceries filled one arm.

Chuck stared. "Who …?"

"Hiya. I'm Nate." He waved. A goofy grin appeared on his face and then vanished. "You guys like Thai food? I was

169

thinking I could make some Tiger Cry before everything goes apeshit again."

Arrianne looked at Gonzalez, who nodded. He looked hungry. She asked, "Seriously, what in the hell is going on?"

Nate placed the bag on the kitchen counter and then waggled his fingers at her. "Your lives are not your own. Oogie-boogie."

Gonzalez chuckled. "Nate, what are you doing?"

"Well, we're racing toward the end. I figured these two should get a last meal. Besides, I like to cook. Not gonna say I'm really good or anything, but I'm getting better." He stooped and reached into one of the cabinets, retrieved a wok Arrianne didn't realize they owned. "See, that's the trick. If you like doing something—if you care about it—you always try to do better every time out. Cooking, writing—I see too many assholes who are just content to churn out the same mediocre shit time after time. It's annoying at best."

"Shit," Gonzalez said. "Here comes a rant."

"Sure, I rant now and then. Shit happens." Nate turned on the burner and adjusted the flame to just shy of its highest setting. Reaching into the paper bag, he pulled out various storage containers. Arrianne noticed sliced beef in a dark marinade, cherry tomatoes cut into quarters. "I get frustrated about the state of the genre sometimes."

"The genre?" Arrianne asked.

"Yeah, the genre. What, did you think we were making literature? Slobber in a bowl? C'mon, you're not an idiot. Shit, maybe you are. Horror isn't kind to female characters, at least not at this level."

"I think we did okay," Gonzalez said.

"Maybe, but the rest of it? Seriously? I can't believe I wrote that dog bowl shit. You think Laird Barron would do that? Or Lee Thomas? Or Sarah?"

"Which Sarah? Langan or Pinborough?"

"Either." He measured a spoonful of oil and dumped it into the wok, followed it with the beef. It sizzled at once, and Arrianne smelled something spicy and appetizing almost immediately. "Okay, well maybe Pinborough would, but you get my point."

Nate grabbed a curved metal spatula and got to work, shaking the wok with one hand while stirring with the other. "I'll admit it: sometimes I'm scared I've pigeonholed myself. *Just like Hell* made a splash, but then I was that guy who writes brutal stuff. You know what I mean, Jesus. Now, I just … I don't even really like gore. It's boring, but there's this whole segment of the audience that craves it. Why? Like, why would anybody be a fan of those *Human Centipede* movies? 'Imagine eating poop.' There, that's your entire plot, and people act like those fucking things are genius!"

Gonzalez frowned. "Nate, you get to write books for a living. People like them. Why are you bitching about that?"

"For a living? Not even close. I'm still day-jobbing it, working overtime as much as I can just to afford the next convention. Shit is *tiring*, man. Okay, yeah. I'm bitching. I'll admit it. Just … sometimes I think we should be trying harder. Mutant rednecks, zombies, fuck demons … shit, just about every last one of us has competed in something called The Gross-out Contest. Where's the contest for compelling characters or solid atmosphere? Nah, forget that artsy shit. Let's just have some woman in a chambray shirt get her ass plowed by a radioactive cannibal with a two-headed dick. Ta-dah! It's the McDonald's of horror."

Arrianne gave Chuck a look, but he just shrugged. Apparently he didn't know what the hell was happening, either.

"You're overthinking it," Gonzalez said. "What about fun? That's supposed to be part of the equation too."

"Yeah, I know. Fun is different things to different people, I guess." Nate pointed at the wok. "This is fun for me. Telling a good story without going over the top is fun for me. Shit, getting drunk and jerking off to pictures of Kelly Clarkson is fun for me. Different strokes for different folks. Heh. I made a funny."

He pulled the wok off the burner and snatched two plates from the pantry. A little too carefully, he placed several slices of beef on each plate, surrounded them with pieces of tomato and cucumber. Finally, he produced a squeeze bottle and

171

drizzled a light sauce over each before sprinkling them with fresh cilantro.

"Here ya go. Be careful. It's spicy." He placed a plate in front of Arrianne, the other in front of Chuck, and then gave them each a fork. "Eat up. Maybe don't turn on the TV or computer for an hour afterward. There's probably something gross on."

Arrianne stared at the plate in front of her and then flicked her eyes to Nate and then Gonzalez. This couldn't be real.

"We out of here?" Nate asked Gonzalez.

"Don't you think we should explain—"

"Nah, they're not gonna get it. I say give 'em a clean slate and wish them well."

"Okay." Gonzalez shrugged and headed toward the door. "I still think it was a rant."

"That's because it was. Sorry. It got away from me. I have my issues, but my therapist says I'm getting better. Of course, she also says I should stop staring at her feet, so ..." Nate wagged a finger back and forth between Arrianne and Chuck. "You two have fun. Remember, that's an important part."

"Dick," Gonzalez said.

"Yeah, kinda."

Arrianne shared a confused look with Chuck as she listened to the pair leave the house.

She heard the door open, and then Nate shouted, "Aaaaaaand, *action!*"

Then the door slammed, and they started eating.

CHAPTER NINETEEN
NATE SOUTHARD
AND SHANE MCKENZIE

Washing her plate in the sink, Arrianne knew there was something she'd decided to do. It was something big, maybe even important, but it hovered just beyond her thoughts, taunting her from the shadowed corners of her mind. She could barely remember why she was washing the plate in her hand. Had she made lunch?

Chuck sat at the breakfast bar, staring at his plate. "What the fuck is going on here? My head's all fucked up. How did we get in the kitchen? When did you even get home?"

"I … I don't know." Arrianne had been somewhere. Had done something. Dickie and Lucy sat on their haunches, glaring up at her as if waiting for something.

Lucy. Her diary. Wally Ochse.

Brad Zeller. Oh, God … I killed him. I took him out to those woods and I killed him.

Chuck still stared at his dish, scooting bits of what looked like cilantro around. "Why is there a plate in front of me? Did you cook something?"

"Cook? I—" Like a slap in the face she remembered the pressure cookers. She'd set up the one in the garage already but couldn't remember what she did with the other.

I must have left it out there. The detonator too. How in the hell did I end up in the house? And what detonator? Was there even one? Why can't I remember?

It didn't matter anymore. The only thing that mattered was ending this—blowing the house at fucking Sixty-Five Stirrup Iron Road into oblivion, and Lucy's curse along with it.

But would it end there? Arrianne wasn't so sure. Lucy's influence had reached her way out in the woods. Turned her into a monster. Made her do things she would never have the ability to even imagine otherwise.

What if Lucy is inside of me? What if it's not the house that's haunted ... maybe it's me. Maybe it's been me all along.
"What if I'm becoming her?"

"What?"

Arrianne hadn't realized she'd spoken out loud, and just as she was about to elaborate, Dickie growled, now facing the front door. The hair stood up on his back, tail tucked between his legs. He barked three times, licked his chops. Lucy whined, hid behind Dickie's hind leg, visibly shaking.

"Arrianne, what are you talking about? Becoming who?"

"Lucy."

"The dog?"

Before she could answer, there was a knock at the door. No, not a knock. Something dragging, slamming against the other side. Dickie had given up growling and was now whining along with Lucy.

Chuck appeared at her side and faced the door with her. "Jesus—now what?"

Nicci's vision was growing blurrier by the second. She could hardly stand, had to lean against a tree. Her pussy felt shredded on the inside, every slight movement pure torture. Blood ran down both legs in a constant trickle, now pooling around her feet and turning the dirt muddy.

Through the fog in her eyes, she glared at the place. Standing tall in front of her like some brick and wood behemoth from the bowels of hell.

The house. Nicci had been so worried about being taken back to the asylum she didn't even realize where she was. Didn't realize those little fuckers had brought her back here.

She felt it staring back at her, welcoming her home, urging her to step inside.

"No," she said, and winced. Her throat burned like she had been gargling battery acid. She tried to swallow, but there was no moisture in her mouth to wet her throat, and it felt like sharp rocks slid down her gullet.

Movement to her left. She flinched and cried out from the shock of pain that erupted at her core and quickly slapped a

174

hand over her mouth. Positioning herself behind the tree, she peeked, watched as a car pulled into the garage.

Someone's living here, she thought. *That's what that fucker had said before. A guy who looked like Mitt Romney was inside. And now this woman.*

It's starting again.

Nicci clenched her teeth and did her best to ignore the pain as she hurried across the yard toward the garage door. It buzzed as it descended, nearly halfway shut now. Nicci dropped to her stomach, chewed down the scream that wanted so desperately to escape her mouth, and rolled into the garage.

She didn't know what she would say to this woman, didn't have a plan. She just knew the evil in that house had to be stopped.

Nicci stayed on the floor, on her belly, holding her breath. A dog barked at her from inside of the car, its breath fogging the glass.

When the woman stepped out of her car, Nicci was going to announce herself, explain that they were in danger, that they had to get the hell out of that house and never look back.

"One in the garage, the other in the living room," the woman said. She set a duffel bag on the ground and pulled something out that looked like a crockpot.

What is she doing?

The woman set the device on the floor up against the wall and then reached into the bag again. But something stopped her. She flinched and jerked her hand out of the bag as if it were filled with boiling water.

Nicci thought she heard a voice, someone yelling, calling out a name. The woman heard it too, tilted her head and listened, and then she opened the car door. A puppy yipped from the crook of her arm and she held the larger, older dog by the collar, dragging him backward toward the door leading into the house. The dog barked, growled, did everything it could to get to Nicci, but the woman dragged it away and all three disappeared into the house.

Nicci slowly stood, biting her tongue to keep from screaming out. A smeared puddle of blood coated the concrete where she had been lying. When she got to her feet, she stumbled, nearly fell back to the floor, but balanced herself on the woman's car. She was filled with the urge to sleep, just lie right back down on the floor and sleep forever.

But she forced herself across the garage, toward the duffel bag.

A bomb. Two of them. That's what they were. Her brother, Sam, had told her about them, used to talk about how easy it would be for him to blow up the prison he worked for, that he would do it too if they didn't treat him better, show him more respect.

And he died. Right here in this fucking house. Torn apart.

"I'm not crazy," she whispered. "I'm no loony. I can't let this happen again."

CHAPTER TWENTY
SHANE MCKENZIE
AND BRYAN SMITH

The second bomb was still in the bag, along with what could only be the detonator. Nicci carefully lifted it, hardly having the strength as she continued to bleed out from her mauled vagina. The blood made her toes stick to the insides of her shoes.

The door the woman had pulled the dogs through was locked, so Nicci hit the button on the wall to open the garage door again. She hoped the man and woman would hear it, would come and investigate so Nicci could explain, make them see that they were in danger.

Was that a gunshot? Am I too late?

Leaving the first bomb in the garage where the woman had left it, Nicci stumbled toward the front door. She had to get the second bomb into the house, right in the center of it. Blow the evil back to hell where it came from.

Her hand wrapped around the knob. Locked.

"Fuck." The word felt like a sea urchin rolling from her throat. She lifted her hand to knock, but something hit her from behind. Lifted her into the air and slammed her against the door.

Her legs were spread so wide her femur bones popped out of their sockets. She started to scream, but something jammed down her throat, shoved the shriek back into her belly.

Everything went black for an indeterminate time.

When the world came back into focus, she was still standing on the porch with her arms wrapped around the pressure-cooker bomb. But some other things had changed. The mind-shredding pain she'd experienced in those last pre-blackout moments was utterly gone, as if it had never happened. But it had happened. She vividly remembered that awful sensation of bones popping out of their sockets. Just thinking about it again made her cringe. It'd felt like her body was tearing apart, as if something had been on the verge of ripping her to pieces. But not only was the pain gone, so was any sense of a sinister demonic presence. Whatever had been shoved into her throat had also vanished. That part of it had been so much like what she had experienced years ago, that prelude to rape by some unfathomable entity. She couldn't begin to guess why the presence had retreated so abruptly, but she was grateful.

But Nicci knew her reprieve might well be short-lived. Maybe the forces at work here were just toying with her. Supernatural motherfuckers liked to toy with people. If she'd learned nothing else from her previous experiences with otherworldly whatsits, it was that. But she couldn't worry about that. Right now she needed to focus on getting inside the house and setting the damn bomb while she was still able.

She reached for the doorknob again.

Her hand froze when she heard a familiar sound behind her. It took her a moment to identify it as the noise a can of beer or soda makes when someone pops it open. She let go of the knob and turned slowly around.

Some gray-haired dork in a garish Hawaiian shirt was standing there in the yard and watching her with an annoying smirk on his face. A tall can of Pabst Blue Ribbon was clutched in his right hand. "Hey, Nicci. What's up?"

Nicci scowled. "Who the fuck are you? And how do you know my name?"

"I have the gift. The sight, some call it."

Her scowl got deeper. "What?"

"I'm a motherfucking psychic, is what I'm saying. And I can prove it. Check this out. I'm gonna count to five. When I get to five, you're gonna put down that ridiculous bomb and come down off that porch."

"Bullshit! I must stop the evil."

The gray-haired dork shook his head, the smirk giving way to an almost sad expression. "Nope, afraid not. Stopping the evil ain't your role in this scintillating drama. And look, evil is never truly vanquished in this genre, even when it looks as if it's been utterly, completely obliterated. There's always a

178

chance for some kind of hokey resurrection, especially if sales are good."

Nicci had heard enough of this insanity. She had no clue who this asshole was, but he sounded crazier than anyone she'd met in the loony bin. Time was of the essence. She could almost hear a clock ticking down to zero, like a madman's bomb timer in an action movie. Which was only appropriate, given what she was holding.

She started to turn toward the door again.

"One, two, three, four, five."

Nicci put the bomb down and descended from the porch.

The gray-haired dork cackled and chugged from the can of PBR.

Nicci gaped at him and shook her head in disbelief. "How did you do that? Did you fucking hypnotize me?"

The guy chugged more PBR. "You know, they say life's too short to drink cheap beer, and in general I agree with that sentiment. I'd rather have a nicely bitter IPA, but PBR seems more apt here for some reason. Anyway, I did not hypnotize you."

"Then how did you make me do that?"

Another cackle. Yet another big gulp of beer. This guy was a fucking alcoholic or something. "That's simple. I'm God."

Nicci sneered. "No you're not."

"As far as you're concerned, I am."

"Who are you? I mean, really?"

The gray-haired dork finished off the tall can of PBR, crushed it, and tossed it over his shoulder. Like magic, another can of PBR appeared in his hand. He popped open the fresh can and drank deeply from it. "Wow, I am really starting to get a hell of a buzz. Anyway, my name's Bryan Smith. I'm writing this part of the chapter."

"What?"

"Never mind. Walk with me."

"Where are we going?"

Smith tilted his chin in the direction of the Ford Tempo parked near the foot of the driveway. "See that car parked down there?"

"Yeah."

"We're going for a ride."

Nicci gave her head an adamant shake. "No fucking way. A ghost-thing raped me in that car. No way in hell can you make me get in that goddamn car."

Two minutes later they were in the Ford Tempo and driving away from the house on Sixty-Five Stirrup Iron Road. Smith was driving. He had one hand on the wheel and the other around the beer can. Nicci twisted in her seat for a last look at the receding house. They went around a bend and it was gone.

"Why am I in this car?"

Smith drank his beer. "Because it needed to happen. Gonzalez declared you dead in one chapter and then there you are dragging around fucking bombs. That's a plot inconsistency on a level with the best works of Ed Wood Jr."

Nicci shook her head again. She couldn't even begin to wrap her brain around this strangeness. "So what happens to me now?"

Smith guzzled more of his beer. "Anyone who reads my shit knows I have a thing for crazy chicks. So here's the deal. You are now in love with me."

Nicci had tears of joy in her eyes. "I never thought I'd find love. Ohmigosh, I'm so happy!"

Smith laughed.

They rode off into the sunset or the night or whatever damn time it was by that point. Later they went on a wild cross-country killing spree. Movies were made about their bloody exploits. Books were written.

Books that were not *Sixty-Five Stirrup Iron Road*.

Chuck and Arrianne clasped hands and leaned against each other as they watched the front door vibrate in its frame. There was a sense of something massive and ferocious assaulting the entrance of their tainted home. Chuck considered dragging Arrianne off to some other part of the house in search of refuge. There was just one problem with that. He wasn't sure there was such a thing as a safe place anywhere in this house.

The assault on the door abruptly ceased.

Chuck hardly dared believe that whatever had been out there had left. Some time passed. He decided to open the door a crack and peek outside. Which, okay, maybe defied logic, but he felt helplessly compelled to do it anyway, even with Arrianne crying and begging him not to.

Chuck cracked the door open.

He frowned. "Huh. That's strange."

Arrianne sniffled. "Wh-what's out there."

Chuck shook his head. "Nothing's out there. I mean ... *nothing*. That's really—"

A scream rang out from somewhere behind him.

CHAPTER TWENTY-ONE
EDWARD LEE, WRATH JAMES
WHITE, AND RYAN HARDING

Chuck and Arrianne clasped hands and leaned against each other as they watched the front door vibrate in its frame. There was a sense of something massive and ferocious assaulting the entrance of their tainted home. Chuck considered dragging Arrianne off to some other part of the house in search of refuge. There was just one problem with that. He wasn't sure there was such a thing as a safe place anywhere in this house.

The assault on the door abruptly ceased.

Chuck hardly dared believe whatever had been out there had left. Some time passed. He decided to open the door a crack and peek outside. Which, okay, maybe defied logic, but he felt helplessly compelled to do it anyway, even with Arrianne crying and begging him not to.

Chuck cracked the door open.

He frowned. "Huh. That's strange."

Arrianne sniffled. "Wh-what's out there."

Chuck shook his head. "Nothing's out there. I mean ... nothing. That's really—"

A scream rang out from somewhere behind him.

A scream rang out from somewhere behind them.

Of course it did. They were in a casino after all, and some lady had just come up big on the roulette table.

Wearing a Black Flag T-shirt; a loose, unbuttoned, white flannel shirt; and blue jeans, Edward Lee sat at the bar drinking beer and Diet Coke, and beside him sat a flabbergastingly large, bald black man who was nearly a foot taller and seventy or eighty pounds heavier. The bald man wore a tight-fitting plain black T-shirt that accentuated every muscle, while a thick, stainless-steel dog chain hung round his neck. With one hand the size of a catcher's mitt, he held a bottle of Mike's

Hard Lemonade, Strawberry Margarita flavored, from which he took an occasional sip.

On the other side of Lee, a tall, lanky guy in a Your Kid's on Fire T-shirt (featuring George Eastman devouring his own guts in *Anthropophagous*) teetered on a bar stool, knocking back shots of some unidentified amber liquid. Beside him, grinning sardonically—and chuckling over some inside joke that only he was privy to—sat a man wearing an Anthrax hoodie and eyeglasses. He was engaged in the process of downing his third or fourth shot of top-shelf bourbon.

"So what the hell happened?" the preposterously large black man enquired.

"They all died, dude," answered the peculiar fellow in the Anthrax hoodie. In spite of the solemnity of the topic, the grin never left his face. Sometimes it occurred to others that this grin was genetically imbued into his features.

"Gonzalez, Nate, Ketchum, Bryan Smith, all of them?"

"Yup. Tortured, dismembered, and sodomized. In that order, the way I understand it."

"Not just that," Edward Lee added. "They drowned in vomit, too."

"I just can't fucking believe it," Wrath James White, the gargantuan black man, whispered. He dropped his head.

Lee appeared suddenly stoic. "Me neither, Wrath, but it's true. I did a Freedom of Information Act request and got copies of the police reports."

"It's fucked up, man," offered the guy in the Your Kid's on Fire shirt. This, by the way, was a young "gentleman" named Ryan Harding who appeared as some manner of social hybrid: one part studious college student, the other part unmitigated pervert and brazen punk. "I mean, what are the chances of something like that happening to four *horror* writers? All murdered on the same day?"

"And not just the same day but in the same *house*," observed Anthrax hoodie. Was he now on his *fifth* shot of bourbon? Jesus! His devilish grin never faltered.

"Yeah, and Nate, for God's sake—he drowned in *vomit*, and it wasn't even *his* vomit," Lee replied.

"I wonder whose vomit it was. Fuck!"

Lee appended yet again the bizarre confabulation: "And evidently there was poop smeared on his face too. Ironic, isn't it? Didn't he have a thing about poop?"

"He had a thing about a *lot* of things," Wrath pointed out. "Oh, what about Gonzalez?"

"Drowned too, like Nate. But not in vomit." Lee paused, as if for effect. "In *sperm*."

"Sperm poisoning." Ryan shook his head. "What a tragic death." He toasted the memory of J. F. Gonzalez and Nate Southard. Then he added, "But noble."

Wrath made an expression of disgust but then shot a quick frown to Anthrax hoodie, who was also known as Brian Keene. "Why the fuck are you grinning like that, Keene?"

Keene shrugged. "Well, since you asked, I think it's kind of funny … but, I mean, in a sad, mournful kind of way."

Harding spilled some of whatever dreck he was drinking right down the middle of his YKoF T-shirt. "Aw, shit, that's not half as bad as Smith. Dick cut off, found sticking out of his mouth, balls somehow pushed up his ass? And then his nut sack was stretched over his head like a fuckin' stocking mask."

"Where'd you hear that?" Wrath asked.

"I read it in the newspaper. They found him in his car about two miles away from a place called Sixty-Five Stirrup Iron Road."

Wrath frowned. "What did you just say, Ryan?"

"Look, it says right here, they found him in his car about two miles away from a place called Sixty-Five Stirrup Iron Road," Ryan verified, holding up a newspaper.

"But … but that's fucking impossible! Let me see that paper!"

Ryan passed Wrath a neatly folded newspaper with the headline House of Horrors at Sixty-Five Stirrup Iron Road!

"That's fucking impossible," Wrath said again.

"Calm down," Keene soothed. "Why are you getting so upset?"

"Because that house doesn't fucking exist! We made it up!

Don't you remember? We were all writing a novel together. A collaboration. It was me, you, Lee, Ryan, Jack Ketchum, J. F. Gonzalez, Nate Southard, Bryan Smith, and Shane McKenzie. Oh God! Shane McKenzie! Did they say anything about Shane?"

"Nope. Nothing. Maybe he got away," Keene said.

"Yeah, or maybe he did the job on all of them," Ryan calmly suggested. "That guy's not himself when he throws on his Lucha Libre mask."

"No way!" Wrath rebutted. "He's too nice a guy ... I think. But-but ...how could this happen?"

"They wrote themselves into the book," Lee answered in monotone, looking straight ahead at his own reflection in the mirror behind the bar. "They went meta."

"Come on," Wrath said. "They wouldn't be that stupid. They put themselves into a book written by nine of the most brutal and extreme horror authors on the planet?"

"Yup," Lee answered. He was now puffing a ridiculous e-cigarette.

"Why would they do that? That's suicide!"

"Really," Ryan agreed. "I wrote myself into Gillian Anderson's house instead. Think I'm gonna need a new keyboard."

Keene downed another shot of bourbon and then asked, "What happened to Ketchum?"

"Yeah," Wrath said. "And wasn't there something about a duffel bag?"

Ryan nodded. "And a note?"

Suddenly, Lee had all the answers. Not a good thing.

"His dick got cut off too," Lee said. "And the poor bastard's body was found stuffed in a duffel bag in the backyard. They say he killed some girl, a hot piece of ass who was fucking the guy who owned the house, before something—I mean someone—got him. Bunch of Dewar's bottles in the bag too. And the note his killer left said, 'Who are you calling "baggage," fucker?' It was signed by somebody named Flavia Something-or-Other."

"Flavia?" Wrath exclaimed. "That's the chick he killed!

185

She's the chick he created in the book! The mistress! The one stalking Chuck! Remember? Chuck, the guy who looked like Mitt Romney? Ketchum wrote himself into the book just so he could kill her."

"Yeah," Lee said.

"But his dick, man," Keene appended. "His *dick.*" Now that infamous grin was stretching his face.

"What in God's name happened to his dick?" Wrath demanded. "Was it sticking out of his mouth like Bryan's?"

"His dick was never found," Ryan elucidated, looking off at some distant mental abstraction. "The killer obviously absconded with it."

"I'll keep an eye out on eBay," Lee promised, and began chuckling.

Wrath was getting agitated. Also not a good thing. "How is any of this funny? These are our friends!"

"Oh, come on, lighten up," Keene said. "It *is* funny … I mean, in a sad, mournful kind of way, of course."

"You say that about everything," Wrath muttered. "Do you realize you've used that fucking line at least once in every book you've ever written? You're like Richard Laymon with the word 'rump.'"

"Well …" Keene shrugged. "I don't know about that, but if so, then it's funny. And so is the idea of Jack Ketchum's dick showing up on eBay."

"You got that right," Lee said. "It's fuckin' hilarious, but don't tell anyone I said that. I was hee-hawing like a donkey when I first heard about it all."

"What?" Wrath yelled.

Harding peered at the newspaper article. "Hey, Wrath, it says the dogs are okay. I think Ketchum would be happy about that at least, the whole missing dick thing notwithstanding. Shit, maybe one of them even got it. Also, doesn't anyone else think it was funny that in a story with so much puking, there was a guy named *Chuck*?"

"You need a drink, bro," Keene urged Wrath. "Why don't you have a shot of bourbon instead of that little pussy drink?"

"Fuck you, Brian. I like this little pussy drink."

"Whatever, man. I'm just sayin'. It might help you relax."

"I don't want to fucking relax! The last time you helped me relax, I passed out and you posted pics of the aftermath online."

"I should have tried selling them on eBay." Keene grinned, remembering. "That was a funny night, though. In a sad, mou—"

"Shut up," Wrath warned.

"Oh, and speaking of eBay, look what I just got." Seemingly from out of nowhere, Ryan produced an old book that read "Property of Lucy Pearson." "It's about this woman who's possessed by a sex demon. You guys should check it out. Your balls will be sawdust by 1936, I guarantee. I might auction it off when I'm done reading it."

"Where the fuck did you get that?" Wrath's anxiety was now approaching genuine panic. "And where'd you get that newspaper from? Did you take it out of the story?"

Ryan shrugged. "I don't know. I guess I did."

"You *guess* you did? Ketchum, Gonzalez, Smith, and Nate get killed because they went into the story and you fucking took something out of it? What if something followed you out?"

Ryan scoffed. "That only happens in horror movies. Never in horror novels. Taking a damn diary *out* of the story isn't the same as those guys putting themselves *into* the story. I wanted to know more about Lucy. I hadn't even heard of half the depraved shit she was into. She's my kind of woman." He toasted Lucy.

"How the fuck is taking out a diary different? Wait a minute …" Wrath looked around. "Where the fuck are we?"

Ryan rolled his eyes. "We're at the bar."

"At the convention," Lee said. "In the casino."

Wrath clasped his head, exasperated. "What convention? How did we get here? None of this shit looks familiar. Why are we the only ones at the bar?"

"Why are you trippin', Wrath?" Keene grinned. "You really should take a drink of this."

"*Fuck* drinks! We're in the fucking story, aren't we?

Keene! This is all your fault, isn't it? I fucking told you I didn't want to be in the goddamn story!"

Keene held up his hands. "I didn't write you into the story. I wouldn't do that to you."

Wrath looked at himself in the mirror behind the bar.

"Well, somebody fucking did. Look at me! My biceps are as big as my head, and I must be like 5 or 6 percent body fat. Look at these abs!" Wrath raised his shirt, revealing a perfectly sculpted, remarkably chiseled six pack. "I'm forty-three years old! I haven't looked like this since 2005! And look at you, Brian. When was the last time you wore that Anthrax hoodie? You look like you do in your goddamn author photo. We all fucking do! Ryan looks like he's fuckin' eighteen, Lee's man-tits are gone! We're in the goddamn story!"

Keene glanced down at his clothing, confused.

Wrath glared at Ryan.

"Don't look at me," Ryan protested. "I didn't do it."

Everyone then looked at Lee.

"Aw, shit," Wrath gasped. "You?"

"It had to be done, gentlemen."

Wrath bellowed, "We're in a goddamn Edward Lee novel!" His eyes shot wide as he looked frantically around the room for an exit. "I *knew* something was fucked up!"

"Relax, dude," Keene assured. "It's not that bad. Technically, it's the *last chapter* of an Edward Lee, Jack Ketchum, Brian Keene, Wrath James White, J. F. Gonzalez, Bryan Smith, Ryan Harding, Nate Southard, and Shane McKenzie novel."

"And that's supposed to make me feel better?"

"Don't worry," Keene said. "You look like the fuckin' Terminator and you're a professional fighter. Anything comes in here, just kick its ass. Anything gets by you, I'll shoot it. Or buy it a drink. This really isn't that bad."

"Not that bad? Not that fucking bad? Do you know what happens to people in Lee's novels? We're going to get spewed on by demons, fucked in the head, have rednecks blowing their noses in our mouths, and who knows what else! I'm getting the fuck out of here!"

Just then Keene began to levitate. Some unseen entity ripped his pants off, tore his boxers in half, and bent him over the bar. As Wrath, Lee, and Ryan watched in mute horror, Keene's butt cheeks spread, his asshole (*not* a pretty sight) widened inordinately, and his body began to buck in midair. There could be no denial: he was being sodomized—quite vigorously, mind you—by an incorporeal erection of mind-boggling proportions. This process made a sound like someone plunging a gas station toilet, while blood, feces, and *lots* of bourbon poured from his bowels as if from an open sewer pipe. Keene screamed.

"I knew this would happen! I knew it!" Wrath yelled.

"Save him, Wrath!" Ryan exclaimed, pushing Wrath toward the bar.

"Me? Why me?" Wrath shook his head. "What the fuck can I do against a goddamn ghost?"

Ryan eyed him with nonchalance. "Dude, you're a big black guy in a horror novel. You might have special powers or something."

"This is an Edward Lee novel, not a Stephen King novel! There aren't any magical negroes in Edward Lee novels. If I go over there, I'm gonna get raped to death too!"

"Well, if we just sit here, it's gonna be *Analrama 666* for all of us!"

"There are no exit doors!" Wrath grabbed Lee by the collar and raised him off the bar stool. "This is all your fault! What are we gonna do?"

Lee merely smiled. "What's this *we* shit? I'm the last guy with the story file. Get it?"

And then he disappeared.

deadite
press

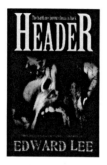

"Header" Edward Lee - In the dark backwoods, where law enforcement doesn't dare tread, there exists a special type of revenge. Something so awful that it is only whispered about. Something so terrible that few believe it is real. Stewart Cummings is a government agent whose life is going to Hell. His wife is ill and to pay for her medication he turns to bootlegging. But things will get much worse when bodies begin showing up in his sleepy small town. Victims of an act known only as "a Header."

"Red Sky" Nate Southard - When a bank job goes horrifically wrong, career criminal Danny Black leads his crew from El Paso into the deserts of New Mexico in a desperate bid for escape. Danny soon finds himself with no choice but to hole up in an abandoned factory, the former home of Red Sky Manufacturing. Danny and his crew aren't the only living things in Red Sky, though. Something waits in the abandoned factory's shadows, something horrible and violent. Something hungry. And when the sun drops, it will feast.

"Zombies and Shit" Carlton Mellick III - Twenty people wake to find themselves in a boarded-up building in the middle of the zombie wasteland. They soon discover they have been chosen as contestants on a popular reality show called Zombie Survival. Each contestant is given a backpack of supplies and a unique weapon. Their goal: be the first to make it through the zombie-plagued city to the pick-up zone alive. But because there's only one seat available on the helicopter, the contestants not only have to fight against the hordes of the living dead, they must also fight each other.

"Muerte Con Carne" Shane McKenzie - Human flesh tacos, hardcore wrestling, and angry cannibal Mexicans, Welcome to the Border! Felix and Marta came to Mexico to film a documentary on illegal immigration. When Marta suddenly goes missing, Felix must find his lost love in the small border town. A dangerous place housing corrupt cops, borderline maniacs, and something much more worse than drug gangs, something to do with a strange Mexican food cart…

deadite press

"Earthworm Gods" Brian Keene - One day, it starts raining-and never stops. Global super-storms decimate the planet, eradicating most of mankind. Pockets of survivors gather on mountaintops, watching as the waters climb higher and higher. But as the tides rise, something else is rising, too. Now, in the midst of an ecological nightmare, the remnants of humanity face a new menace, in a battle that stretches from the rooftops of submerged cities to the mountaintop islands jutting from the sea. The old gods are dead. Now is the time of the Earthworm Gods...

"Earworm Gods: Selected Scenes from the End of the World" Brian Keene - a collection of short stories set in the world of Earthworm Gods and Earthworm Gods II: Deluge. From the first drop of rain to humanity's last waterlogged stand, these tales chronicle the fall of man against a horrifying, unstoppable evil. And as the waters rise over the United States, the United Kingdom, Australia, New Zealand, and elsewhere-brand new monsters surface-along with some familiar old favorites, to wreak havoc on an already devastated mankind..

"An Occurrence in Crazy Bear Valley" Brian Keene- The Old West has never been weirder or wilder than it has in the hands of master horror writer Brian Keene. Morgan and his gang are on the run--from their pasts and from the posse riding hot on their heels, intent on seeing them hang. But when they take refuge in Crazy Bear Valley, their flight becomes a siege as they find themselves battling a legendary race of monstrous, bloodthirsty beings. Now, Morgan and his gang aren't worried about hanging. They just want to live to see the dawn.

"Muerte Con Carne" Shane McKenzie - Human flesh tacos, hardcore wrestling, and angry cannibal Mexicans, Welcome to the Border! Felix and Marta came to Mexico to film a documentary on illegal immigration. When Marta suddenly goes missing, Felix must find his lost love in the small border town. A dangerous place housing corrupt cops, borderline maniacs, and something much more worse than drug gangs, something to do with a strange Mexican food cart…

"Jack's Magic Beans" Brian Keene - It happens in a split-second. One moment, customers are happily shopping in the Save-A-Lot grocery store. The next instant, they are transformed into bloodthirsty psychotics, interested only in slaughtering one another and committing unimaginably atrocious and frenzied acts of violent depravity. Deadite Press is proud to bring one of Brian Keene's bleakest and most violent novellas back into print once more. This edition also includes four bonus short stories:

"Whargoul" Dave Brockie - It is a beast born in bullets and shrapnel, feeding off of pain, misery, and hard drugs. Cursed to wander the Earth without the hope of death, it is reborn again and again to spread the gospel of hate, abuse, and genocide. But what if it's not the only monster out there? What if there's something worse? From Dave Brockie, the twisted genius behind GWAR, comes a novel about the darkest days of the twentieth century.

"Highways to Hell" Bryan Smith - The road to hell is paved with angels and demons. Brain worms and dead prostitutes. Serial killers and frustrated writers. Zombies and Rock 'n Roll. And once you start down this path, there is no going back. Collecting thirteen tales of shock and terror from Bryan Smith, Highways to Hell is a non-stop road-trip of cruelty, pain, and death. Grab a seat, Smith has such sights to show you.

"Apeshit" Carlton Mellick III - Friday the 13th meets Visitor Q. Six hipster teens go to a cabin in the woods inhabited by a deformed killer. An incredibly fucked-up parody of B-horror movies with a bizarro slant

"The new gold standard in unstoppable fetus-fucking kill-freakomania . . . Genuine all-meat hardcore horror meets unadulterated Bizarro brainwarp strangeness. The results are beyond jaw-dropping, and fill me with pure, unforgivable joy." - John Skipp

AVAILABLE FROM AMAZON.COM

deadite press

"Urban Gothic" Brian Keene - When their car broke down in a dangerous inner-city neighborhood, Kerri and her friends thought they would find shelter inside an old, dark row home. They thought they would be safe there until help arrived. They were wrong. The residents who live down in the cellar and the tunnels beneath the city are far more dangerous than the streets outside, and they have a very special way of dealing with trespassers. Trapped in a world of darkness, populated by obscene abominations, they will have to fight back if they ever want to see the sun again.

"Ghoul" Brian Keene - There is something in the local cemetery that comes out at night. Something that is unearthing corpses and killing people. It's the summer of 1984 and Timmy and his friends are looking forward to no school, comic books, and adventure. But instead they will be fighting for their lives. The ghoul has smelled their blood and it is after them. But that's not the only monster they will face this summer . . . From award-winning horror master Brian Keene comes a novel of monsters, murder, and the loss of innocence.

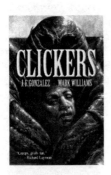

"Clickers" J. F. Gonzalez and Mark Williams- They are the Clickers, giant venomous blood-thirsty crabs from the depths of the sea. The only warning to their rampage of dismemberment and death is the terrible clicking of their claws. But these monsters aren't merely here to ravage and pillage. They are being driven onto land by fear. Something is hunting the Clickers. Something ancient and without mercy. *Clickers* is J. F. Gonzalez and Mark Williams' gore-soaked cult classic tribute to the giant monster B-movies of yesteryear.

"Clickers II" J. F. Gonzalez and Brian Keene- Thousands of Clickers swarm across the entire nation and march inland, slaughtering anyone and anything they come across. But this time the Clickers aren't blindly rushing onto land - they are being led by an intelligence older than civilization itself. A force that wants to take dry land away from the mammals. Those left alive soon realize that they must do everything and anything they can to protect humanity – no matter the cost. *This isn't war, this is extermination.*

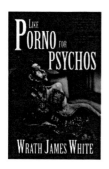
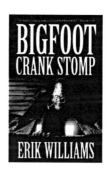
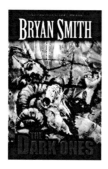
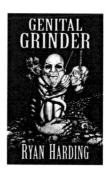

Lightning Source UK Ltd.
Milton Keynes UK
UKOW03f2246301213

223797UK00015B/944/P